Razor Sharp

A Tara Sharp novella

by *deadlines*

www.twelfthplanetpress.com

First published by Deadlines 2022
Copyright © 2022 by Marianne Delacourt
Editing by Alisa Krasnostein
ISBN 9781922101709 (paperback)
ISBN 9781922101693 (e-book)
Cover and text by Cathy Larsen Design

NATIONAL
LIBRARY
OF AUSTRALIA

A catalogue record for this
book is available from the
National Library of Australia

Razor Sharp

Marianne Delacourt

deadlines

Chapter One

Cass

Cass ran a wet cloth over the kitchen bench and hung it on the dishrack to dry. It was that kind of day. A day when swiping a cloth over an already gleaming bench top seemed like the most important thing...the only thing...she had to do.

Back when she lived at home, Saturday had been the best day of the week. The only good day.

Debs and Ricci would come over early, before lunch, and they'd swap outfits and do their makeup and argue over what they'd wear that night, and where they'd go: the train-tracks bonfire, the movie-plex in the mall, or the blue light party in the carpark behind Ahmet's Bar and Grill. Sometimes they'd sneak into the back of Vivio's nightclub, but most of the bouncers had known their age and if they got caught, they were booted out. It only ever worked out for them if the bouncer was new, or Ricci's cousin was working. Cass hadn't really minded when they got busted. The music at Vivio's sucked. She'd grown up with all the House-styles and sometimes she just ached for something old-school and defined like *The Damned or Killing Joke*. Ancient 80s Goth rocked the business, in her opinion.

On those perfect Saturdays, if her mum was still sleeping off a hangover, they'd smoke weed in the lane behind her flats. Then they'd give Rajeesh, the-counter-guy, total shit when they went into the deli to buy gum to hide the stink. Not that her mum cared if she was smoking or not.

Cass sighed. Being fourteen seemed another life ago. She had her driver's licence now. Or at least her provisional 'P's. And in a couple of days, she'd be able to legally vote. Eighteen. Not that any of the wankers in Australian politics deserved her support. But it felt good to know it was her right to NOT vote for them if she wanted to.

And the truth was, that even though Saturday nights had been more fun when she was fourteen, she wouldn't want to be that person anymore. The last few years hadn't always been easy, but they had been better than her life with her mum in almost every way.

She formed a mental list of how much better. (Lists were good when you were bored.)

#1 Getting much better at believing I can do shit.

That sounded stupid. She's always been able to do shit. At twelve she'd learned to fill out her mum's dole forms. At thirteen she'd menu-planned to make their allowance stretch two weeks, and then did the shopping at Coles. But that was stuff everyone did. What she was better at now was other stuff. Like spreadsheets.

Her boss, Tara Sharp, knew everything about people. Like, Tara really *got* people. When they were lying and stuff. Cass knew she wasn't so good at that, but Cass didn't forget anything. And she could organise shit quickly. Into lists.

#2 Tara Sharp

Cass would never forget the day they'd met—twenty-six months ago—out the back of the train station in the Bunkas. She'd never seen such a tall, wild-looking woman before. Seriously. All hair, and bounce. And that was just the outside. On the inside, Tara was like a ticking bomb. And just as you got used to her being, all like, a regular...tick, tick, tick...she'd go BOOM! Blow up and do something left field. In the time Cass had known Tara, someone had tried to run her over, she'd been kidnapped by an actual, professional hit man, and she'd been 'affiliated' to a bikie gang.

Cass grinned. It sounded bad when you put that on a

list. But really it wasn't. Tara was good people. Like…
really good people. Tara had saved her life. Friend, sister,
mum, and embarrassing older person who partied to
Aussie Hip Hop.

Oh, and her Boss.

Which brought her to number 3…

#3 *The Sharp Agency*—specialising in the weird and
weirder. Not exactly a PI business; not exactly anything.
Just doing the strange stuff that got recommended to
them. The leftover problems, for the leftover people.

Cass pressed pause on her mental listing and glanced
around. The office was a pool of shadows and quiet, the
venetian blinds snapped tightly shut against the
afternoon sun.

Closing her eyes, she drew a mind map. A row
of potted Ficus and a tarnished gold-painted statue of
Shiva led clients from the front door straight to her desk.
If she turned to her right, she would see silvery dust
motes lit by cracks of sun, dancing in slashes across the
rich, red, soya-sauce-stained carpet. The building had
been a Chinese restaurant before they moved in. Some
memories never leave a place.

The right side was divided by a couple of large and
ornately lacquered wood partitions. A large statue of
Shuteng, the dragon, concealed Tara's corner office space

with its two armchairs, big screen, and second-hand bureau.

Wal's smaller desk, and couch that folded out into a bed, were behind an equally large statue of Yuhuang Dadi, the Jade Emperor. That seemed poetic and right. Wal wasn't someone you messed with. Cass liked him, but she was kind of scared of him too. Not in a bad way. He was cool with her, and he worshipped the ground Tara walked on. It was just his way that was unsettling. Quiet. A bit—a lot—paranoid. Reckless until shit got real, then ice cold. Hard to figure.

That left the open area with its second-hand white leather lounge and faux marble-topped coffee table. That was for their clients. And Friday drinks. Not that Cass ever drank alcohol in front of Tara. For an outrageous, cool lady, Tara Sharp could be downright...*parental*.

Cass opened her eyes, breathed in deeply, and glanced about. Yes, the detail of her mind map was perfect. The dust-dancing quiet, the whiff of soy sauce in the carpet, the rattle of her desk fan were the sights and scents and sounds of home. And she loved it with every tiny cell in her body. Really, she did.

But right now, she was *so fucking bored*.

Her phone buzzed loudly into the silence.

'Sharp Agency, Cass speaking. How can I help you?'

'Not bad at all,' drawled a familiar voice.

'Tara!' Cass couldn't help but smile, though she tried to sound annoyed. 'How's the holiday?'

'Over, sadly. We're at the airport. Be home in a few hours.'

'That soon?'

'I missed you too, Cass.' Tara's sarcasm was always delivered with an edge of humour.

Cass sighed. 'You know what I mean.'

For a moment, Tara didn't reply, and Cass waited. Her boss wasn't calling from interstate without a reason.

'Everything OK?' Tara said finally.

''Course. You've got appointments to see a couple of people when you get back. Other than that, I'm just logging the surveillance feed from that delicatessen job.'

'Ri-i-i-ight.'

Cass thought she sounded disappointed. 'How's Ed?' she asked.

'Sends his love. He's had a great shoot out on Lizard Island.'

'Cool.' Cass didn't know much about Queensland, but she had looked up the map.

'Cass.'

'Yeah?'

'Been any other calls?'

There it is. Nick Tozzi. 'Why would Nick call here? He's got your number.'

'I didn't mean...'

'Yeah, you did,' said Cass.

Another pause. 'Yeah, I did.'

'Nada. Sorry, boss.'

Tara sighed into the phone.

Cass wanted to...not hug her exactly—Cass wasn't a hugger—but make her a cup of tea and tell her to get over it. Men simply weren't worth the hassle.

'OK, we're boarding.'

'Cool,' said Cass.

Tara laughed, which made Cass feel better.

'Talk soon, hon.' And she was gone.

Cass sighed herself then and leaned back in her chair. Maybe she should just shut the office early and walk to the beach. She didn't like the sand. But sitting at the top of the dunes watching the water...that was cool.

She got up and walked to the door to snap the lock shut. As her hand reached the handle, another grabbed it from the outside. They were locked in a strange, momentary battle for control. Then Cass relented and let go.

The door flung open and a redhead about her age in a short skirt and combat boots stumbled inside.

'Tara Sharp?' the girl with the red curls gasped. She yanked her denim jacket tight around herself and leaned back against the door as if blocking anyone from entering.

'No, I'm Cass, her...office manager. Can I—'

'I need Tara Sharp,' she demanded.

'Tara's not—'

The girl reached behind her back and flipped the lock shut.

Cass immediately took a step back. 'Hey what do you think...'

'Sorry! Can we go over there?' She pointed to the God Shuteng.

'Why would we do that?' said Cass. *Where was the pepper spray? Top drawer? Or in the filing cabinet?*

The girl lurched forward without invitation and crouched down behind the dragon screen.

Cass followed but stayed back. She figured she could take her. They were the same height and weight, but the redhead had a row of knuckleduster rings on her fingers, so it could get ugly.

The girl rocked on her feet as she hugged her knees. 'S-sorry, but I think...*I know*...someone's trying to h-hurt me.'

'Like right now?'

'Like...yes.'

Chapter Two

Cass

The naked fear on the girl's face triggered the pragmatic side of Cass's brain. She ran to her desk, retrieved the pepper spray then scooted over to double check the lock.

Within seconds someone was pounding on the door.

Cass glanced across at the girl. Only her feet peeped out from the screen, and she was still rocking.

'Let me in you little bitch, or I'll break the effing door down!' A man, hoarse and angry.

The girl shrivelled back, and Cass kept quiet. She couldn't see him through the blinds, but she could feel his fury.

He pounded again. The door rattled with the impact. Cass held the spray ready with one hand and slipped her hand in her pocket to fish out her phone. She speed-dialled Wal. He was upstairs asleep. She hoped the banging had woken him up.

'Bitch! Last warning. Or I'm coming in for you.'

The door knob ratcheted around like he was twisting it and one final fierce bang against the door sent the glass panel shattering. Cass jumped back, gripping the spray even tighter. Her stomach flipped and every muscle in her body tightened.

A hairy arm reached through and began to unlock the door from the inside. The redheaded girl moaned softly.

Cass dropped into a crouch. How big was this guy? How angry? What would he—

The door flung open, and he burst in. Big and ugly and mad.

Cass hit him with a full blast of spray that stopped him for a second. But he wiped his eyes and kept on coming, knocking her to the ground with a punch that rattled every tooth in her head.

She fell back, clutching her jaw, having just enough instinct to roll away and avoid the kick aimed in her direction.

As he lurched towards her again, a second blurry shape appeared next to her, swinging a bat.

Wal.

With lightning-fast reflexes, Wal cracked the guy across the ankles and as he folded in pain, gut-shoved him backwards with the tip of the bat. The guy was big and went down like a massive stack of Jenga. He tried to recover and lurch up onto his knees. But Wal head-locked him, gave two precise punches to his face and laid him out cold.

Satisfied the threat was nullified, he then went over to the terrified girl and knelt. 'Police?' he asked calmly.

She shook her head.

'Cass.' He glanced over. 'OK?'

She nodded.

'Go reverse the car up to the back door.'

Cass grabbed the keys from behind her desk and ran through the kitchen to the parking lot. Wal rarely asked her to do something directly. And never in that tone.

The Monaro sat tucked into the last bay, waiting for Tara to come home. Under instructions, Cass checked on it twice a day. *It's not a freakin' pet dog*, she'd complained to Wal, who'd just ignored her and kept rolling his cigarette. Right now, though, she was glad to see it.

She jumped in the driver's side and jammed the key in the ignition. She'd never driven it before, but she'd watched Tara plenty of times. *Switch on, put in reverse then…*she pressed her foot down on the accelerator. The car growled but stayed put.

Sweat trickled down her back. Who the hell was the guy who'd just tried to kill them? And why was the car…

Crap! Park brake. She let the brake off and careened backwards wildly, stopping just before hitting the car on the other side of the lot.

After some grinding of gears and a couple more shaky, jerky hops, she manoeuvred the car around, so the boot was cosied up to the back door of the office. They needed to get this guy out before anyone else came into the offi—

'Cass? What on earth are you doing?'

Her heart started to pogo in her chest. 'Joanna, hey.'

She got out of the car slowly, playing for time, trying to think. Tara's mother, Joanna, though one of her favourite people in the world, was not who she wanted to be seeing right now. In fact, aside from the police, she was probably the last person she wanted to see.

Tara didn't like Joanna poking around in her business, at all. Her mother had no real idea about what their investigation agency did, and that's the way they all wanted it to stay.

Joanna poked at the tyre of the car with one of her pristine white sneakers. To complement her black active wear tights, she wore pearls, and had her hair crowned by a sparkly Dolce and Gabbana sun visor. Tara's mum was not hip, or particularly wealthy, but she knew how to put herself together. She constantly chided Cass about her Goth vibe. It was the only thing they clashed on.

'This is not a young woman's car.'

'I'm not driving it,' said Cass quickly.

Joanna frowned. 'I'm not following you.'

'What I mean is…I'm not going anywhere. Tara just asked me to turn the motor over while she was away. So, I move it around the parking lot. Cass wasn't sure if that was a thing, but it sounded good in her head.

'Oh,' said Joanna. 'Can't Wallace do that for you?'

'Do what?' said Wal strolling out the back door to join them.

'Kick the car over and move it around the carpark. You know, to keep the battery charged,' Cass said, quickly.

Wal nodded at Joanna. He was dating Joanna's sister and Joanna tried very hard to hide her disapproval.

'Hello, Wallace. I expected this would have fallen to you.'

Wal shrugged. 'Tara's the boss. She says and we do.'

Joanna's eyebrows shot up, incredulous at such a statement. 'Indeed. Well, I will speak to her about that when she returns.'

They stood there in an uncomfortable silence for a moment, then Joanna swivelled. 'And who might you be?'

The redheaded girl leaned against the doorway, her arms wrapped tightly around herself. Cass thought she'd never seen anyone look so pale. Like only ice ran through her veins.

The girl stared back at Joanna blankly.

'She's my new friend,' Cass said quickly. 'From class. Her name is—'

'Clementine,' said the girl in a huskily accented voice.

Joanna walked over to her and stood close. 'Clementine. You're Irish?'

'Yes, ma'am,' she said.

'And how did you meet Cass?'

Cass held her breath. Clementine looked fit to pass out. And if Joanna she took one more step closer, she'd be able to see through the kitchen to where the body lay on the floor.

Clementine instinctively stepped towards Cass, bringing her closer to Joanna.

'She was errr...nice to me in class when I forgot my errr...'

'Login details,' Cass volunteered. 'I helped her get her ID verified.'

Joanna shot Cass a glance. A suspicious glance. Like she didn't believe a word of it.

As she opened her mouth to ask more questions,

another unexpected guest joined the party.

'G'day,' boomed the handsome and oversized Nick Tozzi.

Everyone stared at him. He occupied the entire doorway that Clementine had just vacated, his shoulders nearly the full width, his head bent to avoid hitting the top of the frame.

Wal let out a hiss like a tyre going down rapidly, and Clementine cowered towards Tara's car.

Joanna, though, brightened. 'Nicholas,' she said. 'How lovely to see you! What brings you here when my daughter is out of town? I was just passing, and it seems I may have stumbled on some shenanigans.'

Shenanigans? Cass didn't think she could hold her breath any longer.

Nick smiled and stared at each of them, as if trying to read the scene.

After a pause that sent spots swimming before Cass's eyes, Nick finally replied.

'Shenanigans for sure. We're planning a welcome home party for Tara. And you are number one on our invitation list.'

'Oh,' exclaimed Joanna, almost breathless. 'Will this party be at your home?'

He nearly missed a beat but recovered smoothly. 'Yes

indeed. It's a surprise, so don't mention it to anyone yet. Now why don't I give you a lift? My car is just down the block and I'm going that way.'

Joanna beamed and, with a little wave to Cass and Clementine, let herself be led out of the parking lot and away.

Cass couldn't help but be impressed and surprised by Nick Tozzi. He'd just bailed them out of a very sticky moment.

Wal looked at her. 'Open the boot. Then give me a hand.'

Cass nodded. 'Come one,' she said to Clementine. 'You too.'

Chapter Three

Tara

As I switched my phone back on it blew up with missed calls. I hadn't even left the plane, let alone made it to the baggage carousel. In an ideal world it would have been calls from people who'd missed me, or maybe even potential new clients.

But let's be real here!

The calls came from one number, and he was neither a new client, nor someone who would have missed me. His name didn't come up in my caller ID either. That was intentional. You don't identify the Sergeant at Arms of a bikie club in your contacts list. You just learn the damn number by heart. Of course, he changed it every time he got a new burner, so it was a memory test as well.

'Who's that?' asked Ed. My beautiful Spanish, country-grown model boyfriend leaned an arm across my shoulders and hugged me. 'Feel good to be home?'

'So good,' I said. 'And it's just a work call. It can wait.'

But I knew it couldn't, so as soon as we exited the gate, I gave Ed's arm a squeeze. 'Just going to the loo to freshen up. I'll meet you down at baggage claim.'

He dazzled me with his smile and kissed me square on the lips. I had to check myself from stepping back. Ed was my guy. My sweet, beautiful, young lover. And it couldn't last. Nature did not pair someone as perfect as him with someone as imperfect as me. Not for the long haul.

In my mind, he'd been sent to me for safekeeping, for a bit, before the next part of his journey. So, his PDAs made me a little uncomfortable. Like we were a permanent couple, when in my heart I knew I just had him on loan.

Plus, there was the little unmentionable matter of Nick Tozzi. That man had wormed his way into my brain. I dreamed about him. I thought about him. I wanted him. On repeat. But he had to get his house in order before I'd see him again. And front and centre of that was his unhealthy relationship with his ex-wife.

I blew a kiss at Ed and split off and into the airport loo, where I picked the last cubicle and locked the door behind me. The phone barely connected when Bon Ames answered.

'Sharp?'

'Who died?' I said it lightly, as a joke, and regretted it immediately. In his world, it was a legitimate question.

'You need to answer your phone when I call.'

'I just got off a plane from Brisbane,' I said tartly. 'You're my first call. What's going on?'

'Another club's making a move on us. Need you on a job.' He sounded humourless and pissed off. His tone immediately put me on edge. If his voice had a colour, it would have been an ominous, stormy grey.

'A move?'

'A bunch of Kiwis have started a chapter here. We need you to get some information.'

'I'm ... it's not my usual...err...' How could I tactfully tell him that I might not blend in amongst a crew of Kiwi bikers. 'I mean I can do surveillance. But anything else...well they'd be suspicious of me.'

'Let us handle that. It'll be tonight. Late. I'll tell you where and when. Just be there.'

'Bon—'

But he'd hung up already.

I sat for a moment, listening to the hand dryers blasting and the loos flushing and thought about my life. Was I where I wanted to be? Or was I still just flailing around, bouncing from one drama to the next?

I'd gotten into the investigative business when my life had hit an all-time low. My boyfriend back then had cleared out with the contents of our house and taken off with our roommate, and some other odds things were happening in my brain that I didn't like to talk about.

But in two years, there had been change. I now had my own office and I lived upstairs, which meant I was no longer in my parents' pool house. Progress, I guess. Cass had her driver's licence and was nearly finished her studies. Progress. Wal's narcolepsy was under much better control. Progress.

On the downside, I was still in a terrifying game of cat and mouse with Johnny Viaspa aka Johnny Vogue, the city's big bad crime guy. And my personal life was complicated. A while back Nick Tozzi informed me he was leaving his wife for me.

Whoa, there, sir! I'd replied.

I did **not** want to be swept up in that vortex.

Like I told him, *get your house in order, decide who you want to be, be that person, and call me when you know*. I didn't want any man leaping from a twenty-year relationship straight into bed with me.

At least that's how it went in my head. Not quite sure how he had received it because I hadn't heard from him since. And that was months ago.

When Ed suggested I come with him to Queensland on a modelling job, it seemed like a good idea. With Covid-19 lockdowns and all the rest going on, a tropical retreat sounded like heaven.

But really it had just muddied already murky waters. Ed and I had gotten closer, and bless him, he seemed to think a lot of me.

I sighed, flushed the loo and headed out to wash my hands. I suppose life could be worse. If I could just extract myself from my 'connection' to Bon Ames and the Western Cheaters bike club, my life would be on the up.

As far I was concerned, I'd discharged the debt I owed them. Now, I just needed to convince them as well!

I found Ed at baggage claim, patiently guarding our bags, and checking his Insta.

He glanced up at me. 'Good to go?'

I nodded. 'I'll order an Uber.'

My phone buzzed again. No caller ID. Surely not Bon again?

Ed rolled his eyes. 'I'll get the Uber.'

I blew him a kiss and took the call, half expecting a telemarketer. 'Yes?'

'Welcome home.'

'Wal? Burner?'

'Yeah.'

It was good to hear his voice, but not his tone. Normally I could see auras around people, and my sensitivity to body language was off the chart, but this was the first time I'd really been affected over the phone. Wal's voice colour was as dark as Bon's had been but was also laced with worry.

'Wassup?' I asked.

'We got a problem,' he said.

I glanced at Ed as he piled the luggage on a trolley and headed out the door towards the Uber pick up. He was listening, I knew, but pretending not to. 'Right.'

'Come to the King's Castle soon as you can.'

King's Castle was a nickname Wal and I shared for Nick Tozzi's new home. I'd only been there once. Wal had picked me up afterwards and we agreed it looked like a massive fort, with faux ramparts and a gate resembling a drawbridge.

'Sure. Just leaving the airport.' I kept my voice light and casual. But Wal would know I meant I was still with Ed. 'Cass?'

'She's fine. I've got Mona. Come alone.' He hung up.

I slipped my phone into my back pocket and quickened my stride to catch Ed. Welcome home, Tara. *Yeah right!*

Chapter Four

Tara

Ed got out of the Uber and stood on the side of the road outside his place.

'Talk soon,' I called through the open door.

He leaned back in, affording me a close up of his beautifully muscled arm, and shot me a piercing look. 'I want things to stay the same as they were when we were away.'

'You mean, *don't go changing...*' I sang jokingly, instinctively trying to dilute the intensity of the moment.

'Yes.' He shut the door and stepped back up onto the kerb to watch us drive off.

I waved and immediately entered a new drop-off destination in the app. The driver looked over his shoulder. 'You goin' somewhere else now, Miss?'

I nodded. 'Change of plans.'

He grunted and leaned forward to check his GPS for the new route.

In the short time it took to get to King's Castle, I imagined four different disasters. Nick's ex-wife had kidnapped him. Nick's ex-wife had broken in and stolen something important. Nick's ex-wife owed drug dealers money. Nick's ex-wife had overdosed...

I realised my catastrophising had a strong theme and tried to rein in my imagination by turning to the scenery. I'd been away two weeks, but it felt like months. Autumn had left and the early chill of winter bit into me, even in the car. Swanbourne and Cottesloe were revelling in the crisp, sharp air, the pines sitting up straighter and the well-kept gardens perky and bright.

If only the cold did that to me. But I was a lizard. I needed the sun heating my bones for any blood to flow.

The Uber pulled up outside the King's Castle gate and the driver stared down the white rock driveway. His aura, which had been flat and sluggish, pulsed alive in a deep forest green, as though he'd just woken up and found something interesting in the world. 'Who lives there?' he asked spontaneously. 'Looks like a king.'

'It belonged to one, I think. But not now.'

He pulled out his phone and took a snap. Then tossed his head at me. 'For my brother.'

I shrugged. 'Knock yourself out. I'll just grab my case.'

He popped the boot but made no effort to help me,

too distracted by the size of the mansion.

I trundled my luggage over to the gate intercom and pressed the buzzer as he cruised away.

'It's Tara,' I said when it clicked, hoping I wouldn't regret giving my name.

The small gate, inset into the larger one, snapped opened and I hoisted my case and lugged it down the driveway.

My skin prickled all the way. Someone was watching, and the urge to make a rude gesture almost got the better of me. Only the facts that my hands were full, and I didn't know exactly where in the giant building's façade my observer stood, stopped me.

Mona—my car—was nowhere in sight.

But as I reached a sculpture of a herald blowing a trumpet, Cass burst out of the front door hurtling towards me. Her aura bounced around her, alive with energy and a tinge of fear.

She pulled up just short of giving me a hug and slapped me hard on the shoulder. 'You're here.'

I dropped my bag, and ignoring her personal space, hugged her hard. 'Missed you, kiddo. What's up? Why are we here? What's that bruise on your face?'

'Better come inside first. I'll explain. Nick's in there. And Wal and Clemmie.'

Clemmie? I lifted an eyebrow.

She grabbed my hand luggage and walked alongside me.

'Where's my car?'

'In Nick's garage,' she said. Her aura revved into a roiling frenzy at my question. Something was going on.

Cass led me through the front door, where I left my suitcase and bag, and down the corridor. Towards the back of the house was a study. I remembered it from my previous visit. High ceilings, a library on three walls, and expensive oversize couches. One yellow, one black.

Nick Tozzi sat on the black one, and his face and caramel aura warmed twenty degrees when he saw me.

Over by the window, Wal peered out through the blinds. His hair was prickle cut these days, and he wore a black jacket zipped up to his neck, above tight black jeans. I called it his new Russian mafia look.

On the yellow couch, stretched out with her eyes closed, was a young girl, Cass's age, her long strawberry red hair spread across the side of her face.

'Gentlemen,' I said. 'And—'

'That's Clemmie. Clementine. She flaked out when we got here,' said Cass.

Nick got to his feet and walked over. His hug was heartfelt and bone crushing. When he let me go, I saw a glimmer of moisture in his eyes, but he turned quickly and went over to open a fridge disguised as a wooden cabinet.

A moment later I had a glass of bubbly in my hands.

'Are we celebrating something?'

'Not exactly,' said Nick. He'd recovered his composure and sat down again, nursing a can of beer.

'Might be best if I start,' said Cass. 'Can I have a beer too?'

Nick frowned.

'What?' she protested. 'I'm eighteen.'

Nick glanced at me, and I gave a slight nod. Cass wasn't much of a drinker. At least not yet.

'Just one,' he said to Cass. 'A lite strength.'

She helped herself to the fridge and went to perch on the arm of Clementine's chair. I detected a slight protectiveness in her manner, which made me curious. Who the hell was this girl?

'So just after we spoke today...when you were at the airport...Clemmie like...barrelled into the office, asking for you. Said someone was trying to kill her.'

My turn to frown. 'Asking for me?'

'Yeah. But like, we didn't get much time to talk because this guy was right after her. So, she hid, and I locked the door.'

'Where was Wal?'

'Upstairs,' Wal growled from over at the window.

'The guy started banging at the door and I texted Wal to come down. The guy broke the door down. I sprayed him but he got a swing off.'

I stared at the swelling on her jaw. 'Do we need to get it checked?'

'No, it's all good. Just a bump. This will help.' She took a swig and pulled a face. 'So, then Wal went to work on him. Knocked him out cold.'

Wal didn't move or add to the conversation.

'I went and got Mona, so we could drag his arse out of there.'

'No police?'

'That's the kicker,' said Wal finally. 'The girl didn't want them. And now we know who she is, we don't want them either.'

Questions exploded in my brain, and I had to take a second to order them. 'So, what's your involvement, Nick?'

'Right place wrong time. I was driving past and saw the door caved in. Came to see if you were OK. Saw the guy on the floor, and these guys out in the parking lot.'

'You mean right place, right time,' said Cass. 'If you hadn't turned up when you did, Joanna would have seen what happened.'

My heart skipped a bunch of beats. 'My mother!'

'She was out for a walk, saw us in the parking lot. Nick like totally charmed her and got her out of there before she worked out something was up.'

Charmed my mother? *Jees.*

'Do you know the guy?' I asked Nick.

His handsome face crinkled into a troubled look. 'Yes and no.'

'Spit it out, for goodness sakes. You're freaking me out.'

Nick and Cass exchanged glances. 'He's John Viaspa's cousin, Abraham. Clementine's been dating him,' said Cass. 'She calls him Abramo.'

Nick added, 'I don't know him. But I've seen his face before. He runs a boxing gym over in Northbridge. Toni used to do classes there sometimes.'

Toni—ex-wife from hell. By 'classes', he probably meant scoring her weekly coke supply, but Nick would never admit that aloud.

'So, she...' I pointed to the sleeping girl. 'Wake her up, can't you?'

'She's called Clemmie. And she took a benzo. Said she hadn't slept in days because she was scared that he was going to kill her while he was on his bender.'

My heart hammered uncomfortably now. Abramo Viaspa. *John Viaspa's cousin.* Would I ever get away from that man and his baggage? 'Why did she come to me?'

Cass shook her head from side to side. 'Dunno exactly. She thought you might be able to help her.'

'The guy...Abramo...where is he?' I knew I was firing my questions like a series of bullets.

'In Mona's boot,' said Cass. Then she swigged down the rest of the can.

'Why is he in the boot?'

'Had to,' said Wal, laconically. 'If you want him still breathing.'

I swivelled and folded my arms. 'Meaning?'

'He was hopped up on something. Didn't feel pain. Should be coming down now.'

'Shit,' I said.

Nick cleared his throat. 'We could have dumped him somewhere to walk it off. But the girl, Clemmie, well you know...she'd still be in danger and...'

He didn't have to finish the thought. A thin, pure stream of caramel-coloured empathy from his aura reached out and intertwined with my own energy. Clemmie was being abused, and he wasn't going to have it. And he knew I would feel the same.

'Also, given our history with his...family.' He threw

me a meaningful look. 'Figured you might want to have some input into what happens to him.'

Not so long ago Johnny Viaspa had taken a contract out on my life. It was only because the hit man was now in gaol and Viaspa was under a lot of police scrutiny that I was temporarily safe. 'Yeah. Thanks.'

'Let me deal with him, boss,' said Wal. He left his window spot and came over to stand near Cass. 'He won't be hurting anyone again.'

I shook my head. 'I'll work something else out.'

But how could I do that and find a way to keep distance between us and John Viaspa?

Wal narrowed his eyes. 'What are you thinkin'?'

I didn't answer him. Instead, I looked at Nick. 'Hey, I'm sorry you got involved. Thanks for the help with Joanna.'

He nodded. 'You can repay me by staying for dinner.' Then he added, 'All of you. Be nice to have some company.'

The thread between us pulsed so brightly and thickly I almost winced.

'OK,' I said, 'I just need to make a private call.'

'Upstairs. Any of the bedrooms,' he said.

I left the room and headed up the spiral sweep of stairs. The first doorway I saw opened into a large bedroom with a view of the weeping willow in the back garden. The décor was Renaissance style or something oldy worldy. I liked it. Suited the castle vibe.

I checked my recent calls and dialled Bon's burner number. He answered on the third ring.

'Speak,' he said.

'It's Tara. If you want me to do that job for you, I'm going to need help on something. I wouldn't ask if it wasn't...you know...'

He paused for so long I wondered if he'd put the phone down and walked away. I mean, who the hell was I to be bargaining with the enforcer for the biggest bikie club in the city?

I was gambling with the fact they needed me right now.

'What do you want?' he said, more tersely than usual.

I told him the quick version of how I came to have John Viaspa's cousin locked in my boot.

He made a noise that could have been derision, or a muffled laugh. It was hard to say.

'I'm going to text you an address. Come at eleven tonight. I'll let you into an underground carpark. Make sure he's still in the boot and we'll deal with it. Dress up for a party. And no *Grom*. Just you.'

'What am I doing when I get there?'

Click. He'd gone again. *Crap.*

I glared at my phone. The 'No Grom' order, meant not to bring Wal Grominsky. I had to go unprotected into something. I suddenly wanted to jump on a plane and go back to Queensland with Ed.

Instead, I took a moment to dial up my Zen, and headed back downstairs.

Nick passed me at the bottom of the stairs. His aura buffeted mine like a warm gust and he looked like he might stop and hug me. But he said, 'Back in a tick.'

I nodded and entered the study again.

Wal was back watching the window. Cass had moved to sit on the yellow couch. The girl, Clemmie, was upright next to her, head on Cass's shoulder. She looked sleepy and a little out of it. A golden aura streaked with brown lapped at her body. I liked what it told me about her, but she had some secrets too.

'You're awake,' I said. 'I'm Tara.'

She wobbled herself across the room and into my arms. 'Thank yooooouuu,' she whispered as she hugged me fiercely.

I glanced over her shoulder at Cass. Her aura had brightened to the blue of a summer sky, and she watched Clemmie and I with such an open expression of hope, I felt compelled to return the girl's hug.

It suddenly occurred to me that Cass was lonely for girls her own age. Spending all her time with Wal and Joanna and I…well….

I squeezed Clemmie's shoulders reassuringly then gently pushed her back. 'You're safe here, but we still have some things to deal with. Now I just need you to tell me what happened and why you came to me.'

She shrugged and stared at her boots. 'Abramo just lost it. Kept trying to tie me up in the house. Thought he was gonna do me in this time.'

'This time? How often does it happen?'

She blinked, and her eyes welled. 'Only when he has a bad week.'

'Isn't there someone else you could call to help? I mean…family?'

'Tara!' said Cass, objecting to my line of thinking.

For the first time I could remember, I held a finger up at her to be quiet. Normally I was happy to help any person in need. But this situation came with a lot of complications. John Viaspa would be ecstatic to have any reason to feed me, and those close to me, to the sharks off Scarborough Beach. I had to know what I was getting in to.

Clemmie glanced up with tears streaming down her face, but she didn't sob. 'Only Abramo's mother. She's been nice to me. But her son can do no wrong, you know?'

'Where's your family?'

'Sydney. Last I heard. My mum is anyway. Haven't seen my dad since I was six.'

'Siblings?'

'My brothers in juvie, over East.'

I sighed. Was there really nowhere else this kid could go? 'How did you end up in Perth?'

She was studying her boots again.

'Tell her the truth,' Cass urged. 'She'll know if you're lying.'

Clemmie gave a little nod. 'I did a mule run for a guy I knew. First one I'd ever done. But then I got stuck here in the last Covid lockdown and met Abramo through his cousin, John. He told me I could stay with him.'

I searched her aura, and she seemed to be telling the truth.

'Abramo...he was nice at first, but you know...takes a while to find out about someone,' she said.

'Have you been selling drugs for them since you've been here?'

She shook her head. 'I only did the mule run because I owed a guy for a car. I smoke a bit of weed, but no meth. No coke. Not my thing.'

'Heroin? Pills?'

'Nope.'

I drew in a deep breath, knowing I was going to regret my decision, but also knowing it was the only one to make. 'OK. You can stay here. We'll get a fold up bed for Cass's room. But there will be conditions.'

The tears dried almost immediately. 'Yeah. Of course.'

'You do what Wal and I ask you to do. You try and get a job. You stay clean.'

She nodded.

'Do you have a phone?' I asked.

'Yeah.'

'Ditch it. We'll get you a new one. You need to pull your weight with chores. Cass runs that side of things. And no going out alone for the next few days, while I try and sort things out.'

She scrubbed her eyes and held her hand out. 'Thanks. I heard the way they talked about you. They said you had some kind of...gift. Like a witch.'

I frowned. 'What are you talking about. Who said?'

'John and Abramo.' She grabbed a handful of her hair and began winding it around her fingers. 'I think they're a little scared of you. That's why I thought...you know...you'd be the one to come to...Plus they say your guy,' she glanced at Wal, 'is psycho. No offence.'

Wal grunted, unimpressed. Or impressed. Hard to say.

And I managed to stop my mouth from dropping open in surprise. Wal was psycho. In the best kind of way. But John Viaspa scared of me? I don't think so. Whatever stories Clemmie had heard, she'd added her own romanticised spin.

'It didn't stop Abramo coming for you in my office,' I pointed out.

'That's the meth. When he's high…you know…'

I heard Nick's footsteps in the hall outside and he poked his head in the door. 'Hope you're all hungry? Pizza's here.'

Chapter Five

Tara

I took a right down Milligan St in the city and pulled up in the loading zone outside a well-lit high-rise apartment block.

Abramo—the body in my boot—must have woken up on the drive in, which meant taking the long way, ducking traffic lights while he hollered and banged on the inside.

The apartment block had a tavern on ground level, with people lined up to enter. Fortunately, the music blasting out onto the pavement mingled with my car stereo, disguising the worst of my captive's objections.

Even so, I couldn't risk parking here for more than a minute.

Just as I was about to drive off again and loop the block, a young guy with long stringy hair and a wispy blond beard, wearing a black jacket and jeans, knocked on my window.

I cracked it open. 'Yeah.'

'Head down there. Code is 1937.' He pointed to the steep basement driveway just in front of me.

I nodded and eased Mona down into the apartment block's parking.

It was much more poorly lit, and I had to get out of the car to key the gate open. Once I was inside, Bon appeared from the shadows and pointed me to the furthest spot in the darkest corner.

When I got out of the car, I was bowled over by the stench of rubbish bins and petrol fumes.

Bon Ames motioned me over to stand behind a concrete pillar out of sight.

I squinted up into the gloom at the man-mountain. He hadn't changed much since I'd last seen him. Bon was old school bikie. Bandana, long hair, signature beard, big belly, massive forearms and shoulders. I'd learned you never underestimated how strong and fit these old guys were. They looked like beer drinking bums, but they had the smarts and strength of trained fighters.

In the dim light of the carpark, his aura was a solid brown streaked with red. Red, I'd come to learn, could mean a bunch of things. Neediness, trauma, or violence. In him, I knew it was the latter.

My stomach always got queasy when we met. Ours was a business arrangement. If that ever changed, I'd probably become an enemy like everyone else. I mean he liked me well enough. As much as he could a younger woman from a different walk of life. I didn't really fit the mould of how he thought a woman should act or think. And he saw the opportunity in that. But it also made him wary.

Abramo started up again in my boot, kicking and yelling.

Bon's slow smile amplified my queasiness.

'You won't k-kill him, will you?' I couldn't believe I actually said that out loud.

He frowned at me for speaking the unspoken. Then he walked over to my car, thumped hard on the boot, snarled something I couldn't understand and returned to the pillar.

Abramo fell silent.

'Give me your keys,' Bon said.

I handed them over.

'The Nom will take you up to meet Grace. Go with her to a room party. Read the room. Find out whatever you can.'

I glanced around. The young guy who'd directed me down into the carpark now stood over near the lift.

My stomach continued squelching. 'I need some context, Bon. What am I trying to find out?'

He hesitated, weighing up what to tell me. 'Like I said...a Kiwi club has started a chapter here. Trying to move into our patch. We want to know what they're planning.'

'What makes you think I can find out anything?'

He narrowed his eyes. 'You notice things others don't. And Strange trusts you.'

Jake Stranger, President of the Western Cheaters trusts me? I don't think so. 'And you? What do you think?'

'Just do your job.'

I took that as meaning I didn't have much choice. I could, however, still bargain. I wanted something out of this too. 'Fine,' I said softly. 'But I need this guy in the boot to stay away from me and my people, especially a girl called Clemmie. Can you make that happen without...you know...?'

Unexpectedly, Bon smiled. A real smile, not the crocodile teeth he'd shown earlier. 'Always working your angles, eh Sharp. Must be why Strange likes you. Cut from the same cloth.'

Strange trusts *and* likes me? My pulse quickened at that. Not in a good way.

I'd only met with Bon's boss a couple of times. He

looked like a hardcore muso who'd reached his middle forties and cleaned up his act. One brown eye, one green eye, a boxer's build, a sexy grin, and ears full of piercings. His aura was like nothing I'd seen before. Striped black and gold and bristling out of him like spikes. I guess you didn't get to be at the top of a pile of jacked up tough guys without having something special in your back pocket.

'So can you help me out?' I asked.

He shrugged. 'Sure. We can make your problem go away. But the info you get has to be solid.'

I nodded. Fair trade, I guess. 'Will you wait?'

'The Nom will stay down here. Any problems, he'll call me.'

'Does he have a name?' I asked, glancing at the bored guy who'd directed me in here and was now guarding the gate.

'Taco.' Bon gave me a little push and walked back towards Mona.

Right. So, it's on.

Taco flicked his rollie away and led me over to the lift well. Now I was closer to him, I could see he was skinny, and pale, and nervous. He had tiny plaits in his beard that might have been designed to make him look gangsta but didn't quite do the job.

'Hey, Taco,' I said as I got into the lift. 'I'm Tara.'

'Yeah, I know,' he said.

That surprised me. 'How?'

'Saw you at the compound a while back. You met with Strange and the patches.'

'Oh. Right.'

He licked his lips. 'You got Strange's old lady all riled up.'

I flinched. That was a memory I'd tried hard to block.

He hit the button for the seventeenth floor, and as we ascended, he gave me my instructions. 'Go to room 1720. Grace is waiting for you. I'll be in the basement over where you parked when you're done. Come and find me.' He leaned back as the door opened.

'Babysitting duty, huh,' I said, and stepped out.

Taco lifted his eyebrows. His plaits jiggled and his pale brown aura contracted. I had no idea what that meant.

Then the doors closed.

———

'Hi.'

The woman who opened the door to 1720 took one look at me and hauled me inside and straight into the bathroom. A makeup pouch lay unrolled on the basin—mascaras, a glittery rainbow of eyeshadows, and tubes of concealer all neatly organised within. Towels hung over the shower rail and knickers lay discarded in the bath. She was poured into a sexy black number that revealed more than it covered.

'You need more eyeshadow and gloss,' she said.

'But I don't—'

'You do tonight.' She grabbed a brush and began to dab at my face.

I quashed my instinct to elbow her away. It had been a long-arsed crappy day. I had to do this, and it was probably better to just get the whole thing over. If that meant caking on concealer, then so be it.

As she ransacked her bag of tricks, I studied her. Her aura was frothy and blue. Like waves breaking on the beach. I immediately liked it. Standing this close to each other, I could feel it lapping at me. But not irritatingly. Her shoulder length, dead straight dark hair was silky and the gap between her front teeth was cute.

Her boobs trembled over the top of her corset dress, making it impossible for me not to stare down her cleavage. A pleasant view, for sure, but not something that got my motor running.

Every time she moved her arm, and flicked back her hair, her perfume enveloped me. She smelled like heaven.

I wanted to ask her what it was called, but settled for,

'So what's your connection here?'

She paused. 'I work for Bon sometimes.'

'What do you do the rest of the time?'

'Don't you know what happened to the cat?' She put down the brush and sprayed me with an atomiser. Tiny drops of her perfume sprinkled me. 'Don't give anyone your real name or address. Say you're visiting from Sydney. Keep it vague. Blend in.'

Me? Blend in. Bon must be crazy. Or desperate.

She unbuttoned my top two shirt buttons and mussed my hair. 'Bon said you read people well. I hope he's right. If anyone works out why we're there...' she trailed off. 'Let's go.'

I followed her out the hotel door, back to the lift. She waved her key card over the reader and punched the top floor number.

We stared at each other in silence. Her aura told me she was less than impressed to be stuck with me.

'What name will you use?' she asked suddenly.

'Ummm...Clemmie.' First thing that came into my head.

'Call me Shell. Or Shelley.'

I nodded. Why did it feel like I was heading to the gallows, and not a party?

When the lift pinged open, Grace wound her arm

around mine and leaned in. As we entered the foyer of the penthouse, she instantly became my best friend, murmuring random stuff in my ear.

Two guys stepped forward to pat us down and she took the lead on answering their questions. Abdul had invited her, she said. She'd bought a friend like he asked. We were just looking to party.

She lifted her hand and waved to a guy covered in Māori tribal face tattoos standing over by the window on his phone. He nodded to our interrogators to let us in.

The guy who frisked me muttered something to his mate then they melted back into the room.

'What did he say?' I whispered.

'He complained that I didn't bring someone younger.'

My eyes widened. 'Well, shit...'

She squeezed my arm hard. 'Be cool. Try not to act too old.'

I wanted to spit out a smart comeback, but the scene before me shut me up.

The party was well underway—lines of coke on the glass tabletop, joints neatly rolled and artistically displayed on plates like rosettes, with lighters as their centrepieces, and pills in little saucers. Craft beers and bongs littered the bar, bondage porn played on a giant

TV screen, and the guests sat, lay, or danced intertwined, and largely naked, moving to the beat of music I'd only ever heard blaring from night clubs.

I'd been to some good parties, but this was a straight up weed, speed, and coke orgy. I felt awkward about my age, my lack of ink, and my clothes that screamed suburbia.

For a beat, everyone stopped and stared at us. But Grace massaged the moment away by going straight over to the table and hoovering up a line.

By the time she wiped her nose and turned back to me, everyone had gotten back to business.

She held out the straw, but I shook my head and made a bee line for the bar.

Two quick shots of Jack Daniels later, I got up the nerve to skirt around the porn station and join the group dancing on the mat between the jacuzzi and the lounge area. It was the darkest spot in the room, and it gave me a chance to see all sides.

Normally, I found crowds or gatherings a confusing rainbow of body auras. But the low light and the drugs and booze softened the glow. The only one that stood out sharply was the guy standing by the window staring at the city lights, Abdul—the one who had said we could come in.

But Grace had moved across to him already, so I danced and listened and watched the crowd.

When I went to the bar for my fourth refill, I still felt sober but much less jittery.

'Bit slow to warm up, honey?' said the young blonde woman sharing a pour from the bottle. It was directed at me. She'd already been straddling a guy in the corner.

I shrugged, annoyed. 'Not in the mood after all, I guess.'

'Boys a bit young for your taste, eh?'

Whaaat the...? I was twenty-nine not ninety-nine. Did I really stand out that much?

'You should go try your luck with old grey beard. He's probably more your type. He's the smart one. Kinda sexy too.'

She pointed to an armchair facing the window in the far corner of the room. I'd seen the guy sitting there, but thought he was asleep.

The smart guy? That could be a good or a bad thing. But at this point I had to try something. I hadn't heard anything worth knowing yet. Or at least anything Bon wouldn't already know—the girls were all friends of friends, the 'boys' lived at their clubhouse out the other side of the Bunkas in the foothills, and they called them-selves Highway 10 or 'Tenners.' Tonight, was 'Dennis's' birthday. And they all hated the Western Cheaters. Bon's name had been mentioned a few times, and each time they spat vitriol about him.

It hadn't helped me feel any less out of place.

Grey beard over in the corner seemed like he was having as good a time as me, so I took her advice, grabbed the rest of the bottle of Jacks and another glass, and wandered over to join him.

'Hey,' I said holding out a glass. 'Want one?'

He squinted at me.

I pegged him for about sixty. Thirty-five years older than anyone else here. He had massive wide shoulders, and his entire face and arms were covered in tattoos like Abdul. They stood out in contrast to his grey hair and stubble.

Even in the dim light, I could see that his aura circled sluggishly like a stagnant pond, shifting two dark spots around his body that reminded me of the NASA photos of Jupiter. I suddenly wished I'd stayed where I was at the bar.

'Who're you?' He scowled up at me.

'Clemmie. I know Shelley.'

'You expect me to know any of these bitches' names?' He continued staring out of the window and ignored my offer of a glass.

I hovered for a moment and then not knowing what else to do, I sat down on the floor, cross legged next to his chair.

We sat in silence for a while. I sipped my drink and wondered what Bon would say when I came back with nothing for him.

Then grey stubble suddenly spoke again. 'So, you can keep your mouth shut for a minute. You here for the drugs or dick?'

His bold question caught me off guard. 'What do you think?'

My question made him twist in his seat and look me over with an insulting and terrifying sweep. Somehow, I held my composure.

'Not drugs,' he said finally.

'And not the other, either.'

He snorted derisively. 'What then?'

'Business,' I said. 'Thought I might make some... friends. Heard you were all new to town.' I had no idea where I was going with this, only that I wasn't going to have sex with anyone or get stoned just to find out information for Jake Stranger and Bon Ames.

'You got balls coming here and talking about work. What do you do?'

'I read people.' Going with the truth seemed the safest,

and most dangerous, way to go.

'Like a fucking woo woo New Ager?' he wiggled his fingers in the air when he said *woo woo*.

'No,' I said, fighting a flinch. 'It's not like that. 'Like, right now, I can tell you've got some kind of problem in your gut. And that you're using alcohol to numb the pain. If you don't get it treated, it'll only get worse.'

Crap! That had been way too personal for this situation. But his aura looked sick and slow, and the words just fell out of my mouth.

He blinked at me, shocked. And grunted. 'Gimmee that glass and pour.'

I did as instructed.

When I was done, he said, 'Tell Dennis what else you can see right now. In this room.'

Dennis? So, he was the birthday boy. 'It's not a party trick. It's how I earn my living. So, I prefer to get paid for it,' I said.

'What about if I strangle it out of you?'

My entire body stiffened. I continued my fight to stay chill by having another sip of my drink. My hands were steady enough, thanks to this being my fifth shot. 'Well, that'd be stupid wouldn't it. You'd never get to find out.'

He made a rumbling noise in the back of his throat that finally expelled as a short laugh.

The room quieted. I didn't turn and look, but I couldn't hear anything other than the music. No undertone of chat. None of the sudden outbursts or shouts that had been punctuating the evening so far.

Dennis looked over my shoulder at the rest of the room and said, 'Fuck off!' to his audience.

Within a beat, the noise level escalated.

'I'm guessing you don't laugh very often,' I said.

He bared his teeth at me. 'Come out to the clubhouse tomorrow. Talk business.'

Shit. Crap. 'OK,' I said, riding my wave of panic. 'Where's that?'

'In the Hills. Give Coffin your number. He'll come get you.'

'Can't we…errr…just meet at a café?'

This time he belly-laughed. 'Funny bitch. Now, piss off.'

I didn't need to be told twice. I uncrossed my legs and lurched across the room to the guy standing by the lift who'd patted me down. 'Are you Coffin?'

He blinked.

'Dennis wants my number. For tomorrow.'

He grinned and his gums looked oddly pink where his two missing front teeth should have been. 'Wath your name?'

'Clemmie,' I said and spelled it for him. As I rattled off my current burner phone number, I made a mental note to ditch that phone straight after tomorrow's meet up.

He held it out for me to check and I nodded. Glancing back, I saw Abdul's hands all over Grace's bum. She shot me a look over his shoulder and I lifted my head to let her know I was going.

Within seconds, she'd disentangled herself from him and had joined me. She slung her arm around my shoulder and said loudly, 'You don't look so good. You gonna spew, darl?'

I took her cue and gripped my belly. 'Yeah.'

'Let's get you into an Uber then.'

She flashed the boys a brilliant smile and we stumbled into the lift.

Grace hit the button for the basement, and when I opened my mouth to say something, she put her finger to her lips.

We rode down in a silence that lasted until we stepped back into the carpark and found Taco in our dark corner.

'What the fuck?' said Grace. 'Why did you bail?'

'He told me to leave.'

'Shit,' she smacked her forehead. 'I was just starting

to get somewhere with Abdul. You bloody useless—'

Taco stepped forward, as if he was expecting our conversation to get heated and turn to blows. But I'd read her aura. She was just letting off steam. She'd been terrified up there. Like me.

'It's not all bad,' I said calmly. 'He told me to come visit him at his club tomorrow.'

Her eyes popped. 'He *what*?'

Even Taco looked shocked. 'Who asked you to go out there?'

'Fuck-ing Den-nis, fuck-ing Wer-o,' said Grace, annunciating each syllable.

'Fuuuuuuuuuuck,' echoed Taco.

He pulled his phone out of his pocket and hit the speed dial. Then he handed me the phone.

'Speak,' said Bon Ames into my ear.

'I don't have anything for you yet. But Dennis...err... Wero invited me out to the clubhouse tomorrow.'

Ames didn't reply for a few breaths, and then he chuckled. 'Course he did. Now listen to me. You look at everything. Their surveillance. Their set up. Even their dunny. Right?'

'Have you managed my problem?' I asked.

'He won't be bothering anyone for a while.'

A cold, murky feeling crept into the pit of my stomach.

'You didn't…'

His laugh was mirthless this time. And then he clicked off.

Chapter Six

Tara

I was trapped. Something heavy weighed my legs down. I twisted to try and pull them free, but my feet cramped. Paralysed and panicked, I...

'Tara! Tara, wake up!'

I blinked and lifted my head from my pillow. *What the...?* More blinking. Then my vision cleared enough to see two girls sitting on the end of my bed.

'Get off my legs,' I croaked.

They scrambled around, disrupting my doona until we all ended up in a tangle of bed sheets.

I managed to slide up to a sitting position and pull the doona around my neck. 'Good morning to you too,' I said sourly. 'What time is it?'

'It's nearly ten. You got in so late, we thought you needed to sleep. But we want to know what happened. Wal's burning up the lino downstairs.'

The 'we' in this case was Cass and Clementine. They

both had their hair scraped back off their faces and wore oversized T-shirts I'd bought for Cass. Clemmie's said *People are Strange*, and Cass's had Riot Grrl slashed across the front of hers.

'Yeah, it was late. Scoot down and put the kettle on. I'll come down in a tick.'

Cass harrumphed, but Clementine grabbed her hand and pulled her up and out of my room.

My room. I sighed and looked around at the chipped-white plantation shutters, second-handed dressing table and block-mounted Lamborghini picture hanging crookedly on the wall. Living above a converted Chinese restaurant wasn't exactly what I'd had in mind for my life, but now I was here it had kind of grown on me.

And it was a relief to be out of my parent's pool house. Much as I loved them, Aunt Liv had saved my sanity when she suggested moving in here: three bedrooms, a store room, and a bathroom upstairs, a downstairs office area and kitchen, and good parking out the back. It was all we needed, and much better for Cass too. She had her own room, which she'd plastered with posters of bands called *Morbid Angel* and *Exorcist* and scent-bombed with incense.

My parents place on Lilac Street was within walking distance, but well out of earshot. I could have a date over if I wanted to, without an interrogation. Cass could play death metal when I could stand it. And Wal had a room to keep his 'stuff' in.

It also made my business feel a bit more legitimate. An office, no less, with my name on the door. A flush of satisfaction warmed me. The morning sun poured in through the shutters window, showering me with dust motes, and my string of windchimes clunked a gentle wooting kind of symphony. I could see blue sky and smell coffee. Life was not so bad. Despite yesterday.

I clung to that thought as I pulled on some clothes and joined the others in the kitchen.

Wal stopped pacing as I entered. He'd waited up for me last night and all I'd given him was a thumbs up and, 'let's talk in the morning'.

I wondered if he'd slept at all.

Cass pressed a coffee mug and a cinnamon scroll into my hands and she and Clementine hovered as I took my first sip. My kitchen didn't have a table as such, just a long bench with stools. I sat down on one to give myself some space.

'The Abramo situation is under control.' I looked at Clementine. 'He won't bother you again, but *please* don't contact him or any of his friends? If you do that you invite trouble for all of us, and I won't be able to help you.' I said it as firmly as I could without sounding like I was scolding her. I'd indebted myself even further to Bon and the Cheaters over this. Not that Clementine or Cass needed to ever know that.

To my surprise both girls hugged my neck and enveloped me with some kind of strawberry perfume they'd clearly shared.

'OK. OK.' I said, gasping for breath.

Cass let go but Clemmie hung on a bit longer. 'I knew you'd save me. I just knew it.'

I fixed her with a steady stare. 'Life choices, love.' I think I was saying it as much for myself as I was for her.

But she took it and nodded. 'Now I'm staying here for a bit, I want to work for you too.'

I blinked. Work for me. *Crapola.*

'I can't pay you,' I said. And there's no room,' I blurted out.

'Cass says I can share with her while we do up the storeroom, and we can job share the office job. Cass says it will give her more time to come out in the field with you.'

In the field! I stared speechlessly at Cass. But she was over at the sink now, stacking dishes into the enormous, supercharged dishwasher. The single best thing about living in a converted restaurant.

'I'll be able to help you more. And it's time we did something with the store room,' Cass added.

I felt ambushed by their reasoning and the big doe eyes Clementine cast in my direction.

Wal hadn't said a word through this. But he motioned over his shoulder for me to follow him into the office.

I got up with a sigh and resorted to delay tactics. 'We'll talk about this later. I have some things to do.'

I grabbed my phone from the bench as I left the room, and I could hear Cass channelling her wise woman tone. 'You're in,' she said. 'She can't say no to me.'

Gah! Teenagers!

Wal had hunkered down behind his desk when I rounded the dragon looking for him.

He motioned me to sit opposite.

'You OK?' I asked.

He'd steepled his fingers and was rocking slightly in the chair. His aura jinked around. He definitely wasn't okay.

'I don't like it.'

I raised my eyebrows.

He went on. 'Last night, was dangerous.'

Oh yeah. Not okay. 'I didn't want to go, but I'm on the hook to the Cheaters for the moment.' What was that I'd just said to Clementine about life choices?

He nodded, frowning. 'Strange will keep you danglin' long as he can. Youse needs to talk with me first before you do these things. Else I can't do my job.'

He was right. 'Sorry, Wal. It just kinda...happened. And we had to do something to protect the girl.'

'So, what's the deal?'

'They're called Highway 10...The Tenners. Their boss wants me to go up to their place today. I told him I was interested in doing business with them.'

Wal looked like his head might explode. 'And now you gotta go out to their clubhouse.'

My coffee curdled in my stomach. I'd been deliberately not thinking about that. 'I do. What do you suggest?'

'What else did you tell 'em?'

I hesitated. Wal was going to enjoy hearing this part even less. 'Just, kinda, said I could read people and might be able to help them.'

'WHAT!' He jumped up and slammed the table. 'You flipped your wig?!'

My stomach sank. 'It was all I could think of at the time. I didn't want to do coke with them. Or you know ...the other. Anyway, it worked. I get to have a look around out there, give Bon the intel, and then never show my face again.'

'This is Perth. There is no such thing as never showing

your face again.' Wal started pacing. Around his desk and then reversing to the Dragon, and back to his desk.

It was such a small space I could feel the heat from the friction of his steps.

'A completely loony move,' he muttered. 'You know how small this city is. You can't just drop off his radar like that. If the Cheaters make a move, these guys'll know you gave them up.'

My phone started to vibrate in my hands. 'It's them,' I said, swallowing against the cold, sick feeling snaking through me.

'Don't answer,' he said.

I mouthed *sorry* at him and did the opposite. 'Yeah?'

'Tara?'

'Uhuh.' No name but it sounded like the guy who'd frisked us at the hotel.

'Sending you a place. Be there in an hour.'

I squinted at the text that had just come through. 'Sure.'

'Someone will be there to get you.' He clicked off. That was it.

I showed Wal the address. 'One hour. Better have a shower.'

He read the text. 'I'll get there ahead of you. Follow you to the clubhouse. And when this is done. We're gonna have a serious talk.'

I looked at him, relieved. 'OK.'

He didn't bother to reply. Just brushed past me, heading for his bedroom, where he kept his bag of hardware.

I shivered. I just had to get through this with minimum collateral damage. In and out. Enough info to satisfy Bon Ames. Then home and back to normal work. It should be okay.

It would be okay.

Chapter Seven

Tara

My escort pulled into a driveway leading to a long but pretty ordinary looking clubhouse building. Old tile roofing above stained sandy brick walls stood out against the dusty scrub behind it. This was a semi-rural area and if the neighbours were close, you couldn't see them.

That wasn't the only troubling matter either.

Bon and Dennis had both referred to the clubhouse as being in the Hills. But this location was south of Kwinana. Bon had the wrong info, and Dennis had just been lying.

When I got to the meeting spot, Coffin motioned me into his car and took off in a new direction. All I could hope was Wal had seen this and was still following us. This street, though, was quiet and isolated. And from my reckoning there were private cameras recording the traffic both ways.

Crap.

At least the phone lines were above ground out here. If things got heavy, I had that as a compass. I already knew my mobile coverage would be screwed.

'Dennith is in the offith,' lisped Coffin. He pointed to a room at the closest end of the building. Two stocky guys in jeans and cut-off leather vests hung outside. 'You'll have ta give them your phone,' he added.

Coffin hadn't said much on the way out here, and I'd been thankful. Most of my brain space had been taken up with trying to get my bearings and rehearsing my conversation with Dennis.

I walked over and handed my phone to the less scary looking door guy and side-stepped the one who was angling to body search me.

They led me in to a room that smelt of whiskey and weed, but other than that, might have been any office anywhere. Ergonomic chairs, desks, computers screens, an enormous wall monitor and printer/scanner/magic machine purring quietly.

Dennis hunched behind a desk, partially hidden behind one of the screens. He looked out of place there, squinting at the screen, awkward, his aura flattened into a thin dark line.

'Hello,' I said.

He glanced up and gave a snake-like smile.

'Look, ah, it's the business bitch.'

'Does that make you...the office bitch?' The come-back was out of my mouth before I could bite it off. My entire body felt numb. I'd insulted him with my first words. What the hell was I doing? Nerves.

His aura sparked to life and began pulsing. He scowled so hard I thought he might pull out a gun then and there and shoot me.

But with no other option, I brazened it out. These weren't the type of guys you showed your weak side to. So, I grinned.

The silence that hung between us stretched out over my next three lifetimes. Then he chuckled. Like a really warm, amused laugh.

I allowed myself a breath, hoping this was a good thing.

'Funny,' he said. 'You've sure got a mouth on you.' He swung his chair around and gestured me to sit across from him. 'So...what's your deal, Glen?'

'Clem,' I said. 'Clemmie.' I approached slowly, taking in the detail of the room, scoping for any weapons he might use on me, or for something I could use as a weapon. I didn't know if Wal was close or not, but I was sure going to shout for him if things got sticky.

'I have a unique...err...skill,' I said, switching to marketing mode in the way my mentor Hoshi Hara had taught me. *Stay vague but intriguing, Missy*, he used to say. 'Put me in a room with people you want to know something about, and I can tell you things about them others can't. It's not exact, but it's useful. I'm rarely wrong.'

'Right. And...'

'My clients aren't run-of-the-mill people. They don't have run-of-the-mill issues. They need discretion and an advantage. When Shelley told me you were new to town, I thought you might have occasion for my skill.'

'So, tell me what I'm thinking right now?'

'I don't read minds,' I said firmly. 'But I notice things other people don't.'

'What do you notice about me?'

I stared at him a while to let him feel I was making an assessment. Truth was, I already had. Last night.

'It takes a lot to wake you up.'

He frowned. 'What's that supposed to mean?'

'Not in the morning. I mean, you're kind of flat a lot of the time, disconnected. Takes a lot to get you interested. I'm guessing that means you got sent here to open this chapter because you appear calm in enemy territory, so to speak. When in actual fact, you just don't give a shit. If I was a psychologist, I'd say you're depressed. Or a psychopath.'

His aura had told me most of that, but I made a leap on why he'd been sent here. An educated guess, because of the way everyone held him in such awe. No one wanted to cross him.

His cheeks reddened, which surprised me, and his aura bubbled. I'd really made him mad this time. Crossed the line. It was easy to do when you were trying to prove yourself in my line of work.

He got up and walked over to me. We were about the same height, but his body was hardened with old man muscles that made me feel like a jellyfish. The only thing I had going for me was I could possibly outrun him. But not if he had a pistol. And a hoard of men ready to do his bidding.

'Bitch, you're out of line,' he breathed into my face.

My entire insides shrivelled and my mind raced. *Where is Wal? How can I get out of here? Am I about to be smacked around?*

Belligerence flowed into me, over the panic, helping me fight the fear. 'Tell me I'm wrong. Also, you've got some kind of serious intestinal problem. It's grumbling along, and if you don't treat it, you'll end up in hospital.' I was guessing it was his gut, but he definitely carried

68

the spots of a disease in his aura. Mainly, though, I just wanted to trip him up. Before he put his hands around my throat.

He stepped back. So maybe it worked.

'You can tell if people are sick?'

'Sometimes,' I said. 'Or if they're lying.'

He stared into my eyes for such a long time, I began to waver.

Then suddenly, he changed tack. 'You read a situation for me today and get it right, I'll put you on a thousand a week retainer.'

Shite. A grand a week! 'What situation?'

'You'll see.'

I nodded. 'OK. Whereabouts?'

'Here. In a little while.'

'Cool,' I said. 'Give me a time and I'll come back?'

That slow smile spread across his face again. About the same speed as his aura moved, now it was back to normal. Like mud wallowing around him. 'Uhuh. You don't go nowhere 'til then.'

I burred up a little and blustered loudly, hoping Wal was in earshot. 'You keeping me here against my will?'

'Yeah,' he said matter-of-factly. And went and sat back down.

I stared at him, not sure what to do or what was

coming next. Then as if somehow silently cued, the boys from outside came in and each took me by an arm.

I shrugged them off and walked ahead out into the sunlight. Should I make a run for it? A casual glance around at the bush surrounding the house didn't suggest any clue that Wal was close. *Not yet.*

The boys took me to the other end of the house and locked me in a small bedroom. Bars on the windows and a large nasty stain on the carpet did not help my unease. Had they been using this as a gaol cell?

I pounded on the door until eventually one of them came back.

'What's up?' he lisped through the door.

'Coffin?'

'Yes?'

'I'm thirsty and I need to pee.'

He didn't reply for a moment and then I heard the door unlock. He stood in the doorway, peering at me. 'Don't do anything stupid.'

I nodded, so he stepped back and ushered me into the lino-covered corridor that ran through the middle of house. We passed about six doors and after them, came to a bathroom and next to it, a loo. I took my time in the loo, listening and thinking. It seemed to act like an echo chamber, and I could clearly hear voices from the other rooms. Someone was talking about buying ammunition from a guy in Cannington. It was a perfect place to eavesdrop, but Coffin wouldn't put up with me spending too long in here.

I flushed and stepped next door into the bathroom to wash my hands.

He scowled at me when I turned around, obviously annoyed he'd been stuck babysitting me.

I smiled nicely and looked away. Then I noticed something. A key in the lock on the door of the room opposite. This wasn't a new house, but the locks had clearly been put on since. It was a long shot, but maybe the key would open my door as well.

As I walked back into the corridor, I pretended to stumble and fell against the door handle. He automatically grabbed my arm and pulled me back.

'What tha fuck?' he snapped.

'Sorry,' I said as I righted myself. 'My ankle gives way sometimes.'

He gave me a gentle nudge. 'Don't make a scene. It'll look bad for you.'

'Roger that,' I croaked. In his own way he was trying to be helpful.

As we walked back to my little cell, I wrapped my hand tightly around the key I'd pulled from the lock.

Will it fit? Will it?

As Coffin opened the door and shoved me back into my cell I asked, 'How long do I have to wait here?'

He shrugged. 'Dunno. But just do the right thing and in a while, I'll be taking you back to your car.'

'If not?'

He didn't reply. Just shut the door.

I sat on the bed for a bit to compose myself. I needed to calm my adrenalin rush, so I could think. Hopefully they were just trying to scare me a little and suss me out further. If I was genuinely wanting to work with them, I'd expect me to be annoyed, but accepting that this was part of the process.

If I wasn't genuine, I'd be expecting me to panic and try and run. I had to stay cool and see this through. One way or the other. If I didn't, I'd be easy for them to find. The Cheaters would never be able to protect me.

I got up, went to the door, and listened for a bit. Nothing but muffled voices somewhere in the house, and a chainsaw in the distance. I hadn't seen anyone using one when I arrived, so maybe a neighbour was chopping wood. Ridiculously that made me feel better.

I tried the key in the lock. It fitted well enough. Before turning it, I sketched a quick game plan in my mind and committed to it. *Here goes...*

Turn to the right. Nothing...

Shit. A light sweat broke out across my body.

Turn to the left.

Click. My sweating increased. *OK*. *Execute the plan*.

I opened the door gently and peeked out. The corridor seemed empty, so I tiptoed as quickly as I could back to the toilet and locked myself in.

For a while I couldn't hear anything much. Just a one-sided phone conversation that made no sense. My butt got numb sitting, so I stood and wiggled around to get the circulation going again. How long could I safely stay here before someone came to use the loo?

I did some stretching and some meditation breathing and considered my life choices. A couple of times, sharp noises had me on tip toes, ready with my story: *Coffin forgot to lock the door and I needed to go to the loo.* Twice my nerve almost failed and sent me fleeing back to my little gaol cell.

Then I heard some louder voices and a door bang shut. I held my breath and listened.

'Whatya got for me?' Dennis's voice.

'He's got some habits. Today's the *Pie Man* on Main Street for lunch. Then later, Lefty's bar. He puts a bet on, drinks in the public bar until they call the raffle, and then walks back to the clubhouse. It's only two blocks away, and he takes the alley. Usually stops for a piss along the way.'

I knew the voice but couldn't quite place it. And who were they talking about anyway?

'Who does he have with him?'

'Hard to say.'

'Exits? Cover?' asked Dennis.

'Pretty fucking good. Two blocks to the freeway, and plenty of cover in the alley.'

There was a pause.

'Make sure it's dark when he leaves. If it all goes right, like we plan, we'll patch you over right away,' said Dennis.

'Fully?'

They were talking about another bike club.

'Fuck yeah. Deal then?'

'Fuck, yeah.'

'First though...got something else for you. Want you to suss out this bitch who says she wants to work with us. See if you know her.'

'Work how?'

'Not important, but I want to see if she's familiar. It's a small town.'

I imagined the guy's chest swelling with the vote of confidence Dennis was giving him, just as mine was swelling with anger. They were going to test me!

Rustling sounds and the bang of a door suggested they were on the move. I bolted out of the loo and tiptoe-ran back to my room.

I managed to lock up and stash the key into the hollow tube of the bed frame a heartbeat before the door swung open again.

It was Dennis. He strode in and right over to where I sat on the bed scowling at him.

'I want you to check out a guy,' he said.

'Check out how?' I asked.

'I want to know if he's lying.'

I folded my arms, feigning being stubborn and waspy. 'Are you going to lock me back in here afterwards?'

Dennis cast me a dangerous smile. 'After this, you'll be going. I promise.'

'You'll be going' wasn't quite the same as 'free to go', but perhaps now was not the time to push it. And I wanted to see the guy who was about to set up some other unsuspecting bikie.

'Let's just get this done then,' I said, testily.

He crooked his finger. 'Come.'

We left the house through the door Coffin and I had entered an hour or so before. I had expected we would head back to where I'd first met Dennis, but instead he walked straight across the yard to a low roofed garage set off the driveway. It had obviously been built after the house and had an almost modular look, with Colorbond walls and roof. As if someone had dropped a large shipping container there.

Coffin stood at the door; arms crossed. He nodded to me as Dennis and I went inside.

'Wow,' I said, surprised, looking around. Couches, a felt pool table, dart boards and a long bar. 'It's like a mobile games room.'

Dennis nodded, barely listening, his gaze on a young guy with long stringy hair and plaits in his beard, sitting at the bar with a stubby in his hands, and his bike helmet on the stool next to him.

Taco? WTF?

The guy turned around when he heard us come in, and we locked eyes immediately.

Only the slightest flicker of emotion showed on his face, but his aura almost ignited. Instinctively, I stepped back.

Was Taco here selling out his club? Or was he playing a dangerous game on their behalf? I had no way of knowing exactly. My only advantage was that he didn't know I'd overheard him.

I glanced at Dennis. Had he picked up on our reactions?

He was staring at me now, his face tattoos stark under the fluoro lights. 'Problem, darling?'

'Yeah,' I said. 'The dude stinks like a sewer. I can smell him from here.'

He narrowed his eyes, as though weighing up my answer. Then his gaze shot back across to Taco.

The Cheater's nom had fully recovered his composure, and he lifted his beer. 'Helped myself to the fridge. Does *the lady* want one?'

Dennis walked over and clouted him across the back of the head.

Taco fell sideways off the chair and came up swinging on instinct.

I heard the door wrench open behind me as Coffin and another guy raced in. But Dennis didn't bat an eyelid. He just smacked Taco's fist away and went behind the bar to the fridge. He got three stubbies out, set one on the bar, tossed one to Taco, and then brought the third to me.

I didn't muck around. I twisted the top off and downed half of it before Dennis went back and picked up his own.

The instant sugar hit gave me the courage to go over to the stool next to Taco.

He lifted his helmet off it, and I sat down. This should be interesting.

'Clemmie,' I said, holding out my hand to Taco.

'Tacone,' he replied and gave me a slippery grip in return. His eyes gave nothing away, but his aura kept up a fast-paced swivel around his body. 'Dennis says you're lookin' to work for the club?'

'Maybe,' I countered. 'What about you? What's your connection?'

'Friend of a friend,' he said.

I concentrated hard, searching for any tell-tale micro expressions that would give me a clue to his intentions— trying to suss him out. His throat constricted slightly when he took a sip, and I couldn't be sure, but one eyelid seemed to droop a little. His aura was the biggest give-away though. It made me nauseous just watching it whirl.

'Let's just say you're both here for job interviews,' said Dennis. 'Who gets the job though?'

'I wasn't aware I was competing with anyone,' I said a little primly. Then I took that as an opening from Dennis. 'So, what do you do, Tacone?'

He gave a nervous laugh. 'I'm a handy man.'

'Well, my work is quite specific,' I said. 'And I'm pretty good at it.' I glanced at Dennis. 'So, I don't imagine there's any competition at all.'

Dennis sniggered. He was enjoying this little cat and mouse game, but he didn't know the half of it.

Taco was beginning to squirm a little, and suddenly burst out with, 'Where do you live, then? You look kinda familiar.'

I froze him with a look. If he was working for Bon Ames, he would never have asked me that. 'That's like asking a lady her age,' I said icily. 'The answer is on a need-to-know basis only.'

Dennis stood with his arms folded, watching us. I had the upper hand in the conversation, but my hold felt tenuous.

Taco's aura continued to roil, warning me that he could say anything at any time if he thought it would put him in a good light. I had to get out of here and warn Bon Ames that his Nom was a traitor.

But how?

I downed the rest of the beer and placed it on the bar. 'You got anything stronger?'

Dennis frowned and leaned across the bar like he might reach out and slap me too, but the door opened, and another guy entered.

'What?' demanded Dennis, pulling up short.

The guy tilted his head, for Dennis to come outside.

'Can't it wait?' the grey bearded guy snarled.

'No, it can't wait,' said a young, angry voice on the other side of the door.

A second later, a girl wearing torn black jeans and a blood red T-shirt pushed past the sentry, hauling another girl in a faded pink cotton shift dress alongside her. The second girl was limping. They both had grass stuck to their clothes.

My heart skittered. Cass and Clemmie, standing at the door, gripping each other hard.

Before Dennis could speak, Cass burst out with, 'We've been on a picnic near the falls, and some psycho came and threatened us. Then Cl—'

She caught my wide-eyed look and she switched names mid-word.

'—andeece did her ankle. Phone reception's shit out here. We just wanna call an Uber and go home! But this douche bag won't lend us his phone.'

I let out a breath.

Dennis left his position behind the bar and approached them.

Clemmie rubbed her eyes and whimpered as though in pain. 'Please help us!' Her gaze swept the room taking in me and Taco, and the bar, the pool table, and the posters of girls and bikes on the wall.

'Why'd you come in here?' said Dennis.

'You're the first people we saw,' said Cass. 'Knocked on some houses down the road, but no one answered.

We wanna call the cops about this guy.'

Dennis frowned at that idea.

'Where do you girls live?' I piped up.

'Bunkas,' said Cass. 'With my mum.'

'I'll take you to the police station and then drop you home, if you like. If I can get to my car.' I looked at Dennis.

Clemmie started to cry. A low-pitched hiccoughy moan that was kind of distressing and made all the men in the room shift around awkwardly as if someone had stuck pins in them. Cass patted her shoulder to comfort her.

'I can take them,' said Taco.

Cass fixed him with a fierce expression. 'No offence, mate, but I'd rather go with a woman after today.'

Dennis glanced at his watch and his frown deepened. I figured he was juggling competing issues. He didn't want the cops here interviewing the girls. Plus, he must have been estimating the time he had left to set up his ambush on the Cheaters. It was all getting messy.

'Take the three of them back to her car,' he said to Coffin. Then he turned to me. 'You'll hear from me soon.'

I shrugged but stopped short of saying 'whatever'. Once I got out of here, I'd never be coming back.

Coffin didn't look too impressed about being on

courier duty again, but he wasn't about to object either. 'Let's go,' he said to the three of us.

The girls and he went out ahead of me and as I went through the door after them, I risked a quick look back at Taco.

His eyes were bright with fear and his aura glowed like a bushfire. He couldn't expose me because I could do the same to him. He just had to trust that I believed Bon Ames had sent him here, and Dennis and his crew could get their job done before I thought to mention it to Bon.

I smiled, wanting him to think he had time.

Then I turned and followed Coffin and the others.

Outside, the sun had already dropped below the tree line and the house lay in purpling shadows. One of Dennis's guys had lit a fire in an old wheel rim, and it shed sparks like tiny meteorites across the back yard. I inhaled the burning eucalyptus. If I didn't know these guys were planning an assassination tonight, the scene might have even been...pleasant.

According to Taco's description, their mark would be at his afternoon drinks right now and in about an hour would take the walk down the alley to the Cheaters clubhouse. I had to call Bon Ames and warn him.

We sat in silence on the drive, other than the odd

moan from Clementine. Her ankle was wrapped in a t-shirt, so it was hard to tell if she was genuinely injured. I made a point of not looking at Cass, in case I gave something away to Coffin, who periodically glanced in the rear-view mirror at us.

He seemed relieved that we didn't have much to say. And screeched into the carpark in a hurry. As I got out, he handed me back my phone. 'Wait to hear from us.'

'Right,' I said.

Not in a million years.

Chapter Eight

Tara

I waited until Coffin had driven away before I turned to Cass and hugged her. 'Never been so mad at you, or so glad to see you!'

'It was Wal's idea. He saw them lock you up. Short of calling the cops, we had to find out if you were OK.'

I looked at Clementine. 'How bad's your ankle.'

She lifted her foot and unravelled the makeshift bandage. No bruising or swelling. 'Should be an actor, right?'

I shook my head in disbelief. 'You can cry on demand?'

Her eyes widened. 'Can't everyone?'

I shook my head and dialled the burner number I had for Bon Ames. It didn't connect. 'Crap.'

I looked at the girls. 'Have to make a detour. While we're there, you will not leave the car. Clear?'

They both nodded but looked altogether too pleased with themselves.

Cass filled me in on the afternoon as I set my GPS to take me to Lefty's bar near the Cheaters clubhouse. Forty-five minutes, it said.

I dropped the location pin in a text to Wal, with a brief message. *MEET ME THERE NOW.* Then I booted Mona back towards the highway. The light was starting to fade. My only consolation was Dennis's guys would likely be stuck in the same peak hour traffic.

Drumming my fingers on the steering wheel, I tuned back in to Cass's monologue.

'So how did you get out there?' I asked.

'We Ubered out a fair way and then Wal came and got us. It was his idea to say some guy had approached us on our picnic. He knew that would worry them about the cops coming.'

'Dangerous tactic and not OK,' I said.

'I'm eighteen,' said Cass mulishly, folding her arms and looking away. 'You can't tell me what to do.'

This wasn't a conversation for now, so I zipped my mouth and let it pass. They'd got me out of tight spot, and I hadn't left them with a lot of options to help.

'She's smart,' said Clemmie. 'Had it all worked out how we would do it and what we should say. She just needed me to pull off the acting.'

'And you were so good,' said Cass.

They high fived each other in the back seat.

I weaved in out of lanes and finally got off the highway. As I began to brake for the lights just before the Lefty's turn off, six motorbikes gunned it down the middle, between lanes, and crossed the intersection on the tail of the orange.

I panicked. The Tenner's were ahead of me.

'Cass, call Wal, put him on speaker.' Mona wasn't nearly modern enough for blue tooth.

She held her phone up near my ear.

'Yes,' he answered tersely.

'Where are you?'

'Behind you,' he said.

I glanced in the rear view. He sat at the lights three cars behind me. 'Shit. Did you see them? They're after one of the Cheaters.'

'Why are we getting involved?' he said.

'He'll blame me. You know he will.'

I pulled on the park brake and unbuckled my seat belt. 'Cass, take the wheel. Turn right on the arrow. Then look for Lefty's bar about a hundred metres down on the right. Park in the carpark at the front—*only the front*—and stay in the car with the doors locked.'

She dropped her phone, startled. 'What?'

'Did you hear me?' I was already half out of the car.

'Yep. Got it.'

'Good.' After a quick look for the gap in traffic, I sprinted across the lights and down the road.

When I reached the carpark there were no bikes to be seen—Cheaters or Tenners. I assumed the alley was directly behind the bar. They'd be setting up their ambush now.

I yanked open the door to the public bar and burst in, heaving for breath. The regulars stopped their conversation and stared at me as though I had purple skin and tenacles. One old guy, wearing a cheesecloth shirt and greasy jeans, made a sign of the cross.

I scanned the bar stools and the pool table and didn't see anyone I recognised. *I'm too late.*

'Where's the back door?' I barked at the young barman.

He shrugged. 'Whatdya mean?'

'How do you get lout to the back of the pub?'

'Oh,' he said. 'Through the lounge bar and across the beer garden. But it's locked.'

'How do you get around the back from here then?'

He frowned and his aura prickled. 'Why what's going on?'

'Ummm…I…' I didn't know what to say.

'Go through to where the pinball machines are, luv.

There's a side door into the alley,' said cheesecloth guy, pointing to the archway on the far side of the bar where the races were playing on several screens.

I pulled ten dollars out of my jeans pocket and slapped it on the bar in front of him. 'Thanks mate, have one on me.'

The entire bar watched as I ricocheted my way around the stools and dodged the large chook raffle pinwheel, to get to the other door and out the corridor.

Pinging sounds drew me down a set of stairs, where I found a few pinball machines back-to-back in a small room, and...*There!*...on the far side, a glowing exit sign.

But as I barrelled across the room behind the chairs of the players on the machines, one of them stepped back unexpectedly and collided with me.

I bounced off him like I'd been catapulted into a giant rubber pylon, landing on my arse. The other players barely glanced up from their machines as the man I'd hit extended a helping hand to me.

Lost in my adrenalin rush, it took me a moment to recognise the face.

'Sharp?' he said.

Bon? 'Oh shit. Thank God.' I threw myself back at the man mountain and hugged his neck.

He peeled me off him and pushed me straight back

out into the empty corridor. 'Talk,' he said gruffly.

I sucked in a breath or two. 'Are you the only one here from the club? What about Strange?'

His expression tightened. 'Just me and a nom.'

'Do you come here every week?'

'Who the fuck wants to know?'

I let out the very same breath I'd just inhaled in a shaky, slow exhale. 'The Tenners. They've set up an ambush for you in the alley.'

He blinked, taking a moment to process what I'd said.

'My car's out the front. We can get you out that way,' I said.

His aura had thickened to the consistency of molasses. 'Show me now,' he said and pulled out his phone.

A few moments later, we stood by a potted palm near the front door.

I peeked outside and saw Wal parked next to Mona and the girls.

'Wal's car is parked next to mine. I'm going to get him to drive it right up close, so you can get straight to it. He'll take you back to the clubhouse.'

'No. You take me.'

'I've got two young girls with me. I can't.'

'Then work it out so you can,' he said curtly.

I closed my eyes and thought of a workaround. 'OK. Give me a minute.'

I ran out to Wal's car and jumped in the passenger side, with a quick wave to the girl's next door.

Wal gave me a hard stare, easily as ferocious as Bon Ames'. 'What's going on.'

'Thanks for getting me out of the Kwinana place, but you shouldn't have used the girls.'

He frowned. 'You didn't leave me much choice. No planning time.'

I nodded. 'I get that. Sorry.' And I was. I really hadn't been making it easy for him lately.

'I need to go to the Cheaters clubhouse with Bon. One of their guys is informing on them.'

'Taco?' he asked.

'You know him?'

'I know who he is. Saw him arrive there. Wondered whose side he was playing.'

'Can you take the girls home? They shouldn't be out here.'

He gave me the same 'I'm not a babysitter' glare I'd seen Coffin use. 'Cass has her licence. She can take my car home. I'll come with you.'

He wasn't budging on this, I could tell.

'Fine,' I said. 'But we have to move now. 'I'll drive my

car up to the door and get him. We'll swap over there.'
I jumped out and hustled over to my own car door
window.

Cass cracked it open. She and Clementine had been
sharing a packet of potato crisps, and the crumbs lay
sprinkled across the seat.

'Drive Mona over to the front door, then you and
Clementine will take Wal's car and go home.'

I expected her to argue, or ask a million questions,
but she just nodded and climbed into the driver's seat.
Sometimes she surprised me.

I followed both cars across the parking lot to the
hotel entrance and waited for them to do the swap.
I gave her shoulder a squeeze as she walked past me
heading to Wal's car.

'Thanks,' I said. 'Drive safe, hon.'

Clementine joined her, hugging her arm. 'She will.
She's an awesome driver.'

The smile they exchanged was so sweet I wanted to
cry.

'I'll see you both later.'

They got into Wal's car and he in turn climbed into
my back seat. I motioned to Bon Ames who was still
talking on his phone in the foyer. He strode out
immediately and folded his bulk into the passenger seat

next to me. After a curt nod to Wal in the back, he crossed his arms. 'Get moving,' he said. 'Strange is waiting.'

Chapter Nine

Tara

I pointed Mona back out onto the road and turned immediately right towards the intersection that would take me to the clubhouse. Cass turned left behind me, to go in the opposite direction. The tension in my shoulders eased as our cars parted. At least they were out of harm's way.

As we flashed down the side streets, I thought I caught a glimpse of a group of bikes parked at the end of a cul-de-sac. But they also might have just belonged to the homeowners. Where the Tenners had gathered was anyone's guess.

None of us spoke until I pulled up at the clubhouse gates and Bon pulled out his phone.

'Open up,' he said.

The gate swung inward, and I drove straight up to the first house's paved driveway. The second house lay beyond the swimming pool, and I'd never been in there.

The first house had been converted into their clubhouse, so I guessed the second was their accommodation. The Western Cheaters resort!

As we pulled up, Bon glanced over his shoulder at Wal. 'You carryin', Grom?'

Wal grunted and shrugged.

'Best you stay in the car then.'

Wal didn't look happy, but it wasn't a suggestion. At least they weren't going to frisk him.

'She'll be back out in a bit,' he added.

I was surprised Bon was proffering this kind of information. But even the Cheater's Sergeant at Arms seemed to have respect for my security chief.

'In one piece,' said Wal.

Bon Ames nodded. Just once. It didn't inspire me with confidence.

I followed him into the house. Their front room had been converted into a lounge, dotted with bar stools, second-hand couches, and mismatched side tables. A jukebox squatted between a massive set of speakers, and a giant screen hooked up to an Xbox with multiple controllers stacked next to it, lay along one wall. The contingent of bikers congregated around the bar, but no one was drinking. A pensiveness hung over the room like they were expecting to be told they were going to war.

I felt like a harbinger, and too many sets of eyes watched me walk up the stairs with Bon. On the couple of occasions I'd come here before, the games room had never been so crowded.

When I entered their upstairs meeting room, Jake Stranger—Strange—turned from the window to greet me. I felt the little shock of energy that zapped me every time I saw him. He did too, I know, because I saw it streak out like a little lighting strike, and when it hit him, he flinched.

The only other person I'd ever had such a physical spark with, was Nick Tozzi, and that had already gotten me into way too much bother. There was no way in hell I would ever act on this little bit of inexplicable chemistry.

Besides the fact that Strange was the president of a bunch of men whose behaviour was not to my liking, he had a downright scary girlfriend.

All this flashed through my mind as I stopped just short of the table, keeping it between us.

'Tara,' Strange said, with a flutter of his odd-coloured eyes. 'What d'ya know?'

Bon Ames shut the door behind us and gave me a slight shove sending me around closer to his boss.

'A group of the Tenners are in the alley behind the bar. They know Bon's routine and were going to...' The truth is I didn't know exactly what they were going to do.

'How do they know? They been watching us?'

This is the part I'd been dreading. Taco was a double-dealing liar, but he might have had his reasons. And I didn't have to use much imagination to know what the Cheaters did with people who betrayed them like this. 'I went there, and they had me locked up in a room there for a while to stop me from leaving. But I managed to get out and I overheard a conversation. One of your guys wants to patch over to them, so to show his loyalty, he told them about Bon's going to the bar every week.'

Strange slammed his fist on the table and cast his sergeant a ferocious look. 'I told you that barmaid was bad news, Bon.'

My eyes widened. Bon was at Lefty's every week because of a barmaid! It shouldn't have surprised me, but it did.

Strange shot me a look. 'Who was it?'

'I don't know,' I said, holding his stare. 'I was hiding...' I squirmed a bit, '...in the loo and the echo was bad. I just know it was one of your guys, from what he said.'

I couldn't tell if Strange believed me or not, but his aura bristled with black and gold tiger stripes of agitation. Stopping a Cheater's member getting killed was all I'd really intended to do. I didn't want to be responsible for Taco being punished, sleazy as the dude was. Strange and Bon would have to work out on their own who their traitor was.

Bon's hand came down hard on my shoulder. 'You're not protecting anyone, Sharp, are you?'

I scowled at him, refusing to wince. 'And why the hell would I do that? I came here to warn you, didn't I? Jees, what more do you want?'

Bon Ames and Strange exchanged looks.

'Bring her with us,' said Bon.

'No. She stays here,' said Strange.

'Bring me where? I'm not going into an alleyway with two rival gangs.'

The men continued to lock eyes, until Bon visibly capitulated. The room filled with their opposing energies, suffocating me.

'Stay here until we get back. We'll take Grom with us. Make sure you do,' Bon said to me.

Strange nodded. 'Let's go.'

I walked between them down the stairs, Bon close behind me. Then I peeled off to stand near the jukebox with my back to the wall.

Bon Ames went straight behind the bar and tapped

his finger a few times on the tablet resting against two large beer mugs. I jumped a foot when a song suddenly blared out of the giant speakers next to me, the sound so loud it took me a bit to recognise its wailing heavy metal vibe. 'Motorcycle Man' by Saxon. I knew it well.

Within minutes, every Cheater in the compound and some of their partners flooded through the door and crowded around, responding to the club's call to arms.

I spotted Grace leaning against a big guy with a black beard and shaved head. They both wore sunglasses even though it was dark. Strange's woman was there too, next to her man, thumbs hooked through her jean loops, ink black hair pulled tight in a pony tail, eyes heavy with eyeliner.

The Sergeant at Arms killed the music and bellowed 'Quiet!' to those who immediately began shouting questions.

Strange vaulted up onto the bar to address them.

'We've just heard that the Tenners are waiting in the alley behind Lefty's to ambush Bon. We're going to come from behind and surprise them. All the Patches need to get to the gate now. Nom's will stay here with the women and prepare the clubhouse.' He looked at Bon and nodded over towards the corridor. 'Devo, help with the gear.'

Grace's man straightened and disappeared into the corridor with Bon Ames.

Strange began to do a head count. 'Where's Taco,' he said.

I tried to shrink back into the wall.

'Working back,' yelled someone.

'Call him in,' Strange ordered. 'I want everyone inside tonight. Let's go.'

The Patches moved quickly, like it was a military drill, and soon the sound of bike engines drowned out anything else.

That left me in the rec room with a few Noms and a bunch of women. Now the crowd had thinned, Strange's woman noticed me and pointed.

'What the fuck's she doing here?' she growled to the closest Nom.

When he shrugged, she started towards me, but Grace intercepted her, grabbing her arm, and muttering in her ear.

That gave me enough time to head to the door and step outside.

Exhaust fumes choked up the compound, as the bikes mustered around the gate. I didn't know what Strange's plan was, but the Tenners were going to hear them coming a mile away.

Bon Ames and Devo—Grace's man—threaded between the riders letting them dip into the sacks they were carrying. Each of them took either a pistol or a knife. Mostly they took both.

The process went like clockwork. Not their first rodeo.

Bon made his own selection and tucked it into his jacket. Then he went over to my car and spoke to Wal for a bit.

Wal nodded and got into the driver's seat. He started the engine and pulled Mona around behind the bikes, ready to follow them out. If he saw me, he made no indication.

I wanted to run over there and beg them to stop, but that would have been ludicrous. I'd set in motion something I couldn't control. Now I had to deal with the consequences. Not a great feeling.

I gave myself a mental shake. As long as Cass and Clementine were well away from trouble, I was okay...I mean...I had to be. I'd brought the rest of it on myself.

No one seemed to notice me, so I sidled around the edge of the building, away from the noise, and called Ed. He picked up immediately.

'Hey beautiful. I miss you,' he said.

My eyes moistened. 'It's only been a day.'

'Felt like a rushed goodbye after the airport. Say… what's that noise?'

I tried to cover the phone speaker as the bikes roared to a crescendo and peeled out through the gates.

'Just traffic,' I said finally, when the noise lessened.

He hesitated, not buying my explanation. 'Everything alright?'

Normally I kept my work from Ed, but today…'Not so peachy. Just wanted to hear your voice.'

'What can I do?' he said, immediately concerned.

'Nothing. It's OK. Just talk to me for a bit. What job are you on?'

He began to talk about his gig; how a model hadn't turned up, and the photographer was so high he'd put his camera in the fridge and tried to shoot film with a TV remote.

I listened to him without listening, distracted by the last of the bikes headed out the gate, and Strange's girlfriend began barking at the Noms to shift furniture around as a barricade.

I walked away from both sounds in a circuit past the swimming pool and the garages that lay in between the two houses, and over to a dark section of the fence.

I could leg it, if I could get past the Noms guarding the gate, but what then? I didn't want them trying to use

Wal against me.

'Hey, come back inside,' someone called out. 'We need to get ready.'

Maybe Grace? But I didn't look back, just kept up my wandering around the perimeter. They'd have to drag me kicking and screaming if they wanted to lock me in with...I suddenly realised I didn't even know Strange's woman's name. Our last meeting hadn't been cordial enough to ask.

'Call me back if you need anything. I'm just about done here anyway,' said Ed, winding up his story. Then he added. 'Will I see you tonight?'

'I'll check in later,' I reassured him. 'We'll make plans.'

'Fine.'

We both lingered a bit and the silence stretched.

'I love you,' he said finally, and hung up.

Say what? I sagged into the Colourbond fence for support. Holy hell, I hadn't...I didn't...I banged my head gently against the cladding and kicked at couple of drink crates lying on the ground.

No! Not love! What can I do with love? He was too young. I was too old. And my last experience of love had stripped me of my dignity and my furnishings. Plus, there was the Nick Tozzi giant old spanner.

Jamming my phone back in my pocket, I grabbed the plastic crates and stacked them. Then I set them against the fence and hopped up. With that extra height, I could just see over the top of the cladding between the extra barricade of wire running around the top. Not barbed wire, but a chicken mesh that would slow anyone down.

The street lights vaguely lit a few shadowy cars parked along the kerbs. I listened hard. Lefty's was only a couple of blocks away. If anything bad had gone down, surely I'd hear the drama?

For a while, nothing seemed out of the ordinary. But then I heard some shouts and the whoof of a collision in the distance. Like a car crash. And a pop. Either a backfire or a gun shot.

At least that would alert the cops.

As I watched and listened for more clues to what was going down, a couple of cars cruised past the compound—both large, dark sedans. Their closeness to each other bothered me. I had some sense of recognition I couldn't place. This wasn't a casual drive by. They appeared to be casing the clubhouse.

I thought about going back and telling Strange's lady what I'd seen. But chances were she'd just laugh at me. Or put me under some sort of house arrest.

The cars disappeared around the block, and after a

bit, I climbed down and continued my wander around the compound. Nothing I could do but wait. And it was killing me.

I tried calling Cass. She didn't pick up.

I thought about calling Nick too, then remembered Ed's declaration of love and felt guilty.

My ruminations carried me around the side of the second house and to the garage behind it. The roller door was down and padlocked, and the side door was bolted from the outside. This was a place set up to keep things in.

I glanced about. It was fully dark now. Only the floodlights around the pool and near the gate cast any light. No one else seemed to be outside.

On impulse, I walked to the smaller door of the garage and undid the bolt. Maybe I'd find a ladder inside that I could use to get over the wall.

The door swung outward when I released the bolt, and I fumbled for my phone torch as I stepped inside. But as I tapped it on, something chopped painfully hard at my wrist and my phone skittered onto the concrete floor.

Someone!

In reflex, I lifted my other arm to protect my face, and though it deflected the punch that followed, I folded like a pack of cards and lay there stunned.

'Keep still or I'll break your fucking neck,' a man's voice growled in my ear as he patted me down.

He clearly didn't know who he was talking to.

Chapter Ten

Tara

The moment my shock waned, I launched into full combat. Lashing about with my arms and legs, I managed to connect with his chin.

He hit the deck next to me and I scrambled on top of him. We tangled up, rolling back and forth. He was stronger and bigger, but I managed to let loose with a desperate right hook.

It only connected with his shoulder though, and he laughed and spun me underneath him. His hands immediately shifted to my neck, and he began to squeeze.

The choking pressure cut off my breath and I kicked up on reflex, but the lack of oxygen took the sting from my attack.

'Get off her, you piece of crap!' roared a voice above us. 'Or I'll blow your brains all the way to Sydney.'

His grip immediately eased. He rolled off, leaving me coughing and gasping.

I squinted up at the light that had flicked on and saw two blurry shapes standing at arm's length. After a few blinks, I saw Grace. She was a few paces behind Jake Strange's old lady, who had a semi-auto tucked into her shoulder like she was a Special Forces veteran.

I blinked one more time to be sure I wasn't hallucinating.

'Get up nice and slow,' she said to my assailant. 'And back up.'

I looked at him for the first time and felt vomit creep up the back of my throat. *Abramo!* Alive and well.

'Get your carcass outside,' Jake's old lady growled at me.

That got me scrambling up and out into the night.

Both women backed out after me, and Grace locked and padlocked the door.

Abramo immediately began kicking and shouting, but the door seemed to be reinforced.

'Thanks,' I said shakily. 'I didn't know there was anyone in there.' I dusted off my hand and held it out to Jake's old lady. 'I'm Tara.'

The woman dropped the rifle from her shoulder and ignored my hand. 'I'm Angel,' she said. 'Get your arse back into the rec room. We're under siege rules.'

She marched off ahead and left Grace to escort me back.

'Siege rules?' I asked, dumbly.

'We have rules when somethin's going down outside. Club law. And Angel's in charge,' said Grace.

'What's that mean?'

She shrugged. 'Just try and keep a low profile in case she decides to use that hardware on you.'

I glanced at her, but in the near-dark, it was hard to tell if she was joking.

She grabbed me by the arm and hurried me into the house. As we crossed the threshold, a Nom slammed the door behind us and pulled a steel mesh shutter across it.

Not that I'd been in the house many times, but I sure hadn't noticed that little Fort Knox add-on before.

As we entered the rec room, all the windows appeared to be boarded up the same way. The TV on the wall blared with a quiz game and the other women had dragged all the tables and chairs out of the way and were sitting on bedrolls. I guess that meant I was staying the night.

Angel was over peering at the smorgasbord of weapons lying on the bar. The rest of the Noms had crowded around a ladder that went up to a manhole.

'What are they doing?' I asked Grace.

'Securing the roof space,' she said, as if it was a stupid question. Then she left me to go and help roll the remainder of the bedding out.

I stood uncertain for a moment and then made a decision. 'Angel!' I said loudly.

The whole room stopped dead, and everyone stared at me. I kept my attention on her.

Her thick eyeliner stood out starkly on her pale face. She looked tired but focussed. I knew that look. And now I could see properly, her aura was telling its own story. It ran around her in thin blue stripes, circling fast and intensely, but not at full throttle. When I'd called her name, it had spasmed for a moment.

'What?' she said.

I swallowed. 'Look it may be nothing, but I saw some cars go past earlier. They stuck super close to each other like they were casing the compound.'

She frowned and stalked over, the rifle still slung across her shoulders.

I took an involuntary step back.

'What kind of cars?' she demanded.

I told her what I'd seen. 'They looked familiar, but I can't work out why?' My phone buzzed in my pocket. I pulled it out, and caller ID said it was Cass. 'I just have to take this,' I said.

She flicked her hair and stayed right in front of me, listening intently.

'Cass,' I said. 'Everything alright?'

'I'm at the Cheaters gate. Can you let me in?'

'What!? Why? Where's Clemmie?'

'Please come now, or—' She hung up abruptly.

I ran straight past Angel to the door and began rattling the security screen to get out.

A Nom appeared and grabbed my hand to stop me. I swung a punch. 'Let me out of here. Now!'

Angel shoved the gun barrel in my back. 'Settle down,' she said. 'What's going on.'

I stiffened. 'My…err…sister's at the gate. In trouble.'

'Why'd she come here?'

'I don't know. She was at Lefty's, and I sent her home. Something's happened.'

The barrel withdrew from my back. 'Turn around.'

I slowly faced her, and she waved the gun towards the CCTV screen on the wall near the bar.

Together we crabbed sideways to it, and she squinted up. 'That her?'

I looked at the waifish figure standing under the floodlight at the gate and my heart thumped painfully. 'Yes. She got me out of the tight spot up at the Tenner's clubhouse today, so I could come here. I sent her home afterwards. Something must have gone wrong.'

Angel nodded slowly, like she was mentally thumbing

through a number of courses of action. Finally, she said, 'Pigs! Mason! Open the door and come.'

She said it like a person used to no opposition.

The Noms jumped to unlock the screens and the four of us left the house.

I sprinted ahead to the gate and called out. 'Cass, I'm coming.'

'Tara?'

'Hurry up!' I yelled back at Angel and the Noms.

But they took their time, looking around, as though they expected someone to jump out of the darkest shadows near the fence.

One of them keyed the alarm off to open the door gate. I stood close enough to him to smell the beer and cigarettes on his breath.

Angel was behind us with the rifle raised. I thought she was being dramatic, but even so, she was a hard-arse piece of work. I felt a tingle of either admiration, or maybe it was fear that my back was exposed to a psychotic woman holding a lethal weapon.

As the gate opened, I practically fell outside the gate to grab Cass, scooping her up in my arms. But before I could draw her back into the compound, a blunt object pressed into the back of my skull.

'Stand still bitch,' said a chillingly familiar voice.

'Tell them to bring Abramo out now, or I'm gonna take you and your girl for a long ride out to Serpentine dam.'

John Viaspa!

He nudged the gun forcefully. Next to me, Cass whimpered.

I squeezed her hand and then let go.

'Tell her!' he said.

I could see Angel through the crack in the door. She knew something was up, but she hadn't given the order to shut the gate on me yet.

'Angel,' I said as calmly as I could. 'John Viaspa has a gun to my head.'

The rifle twitched in her grip. 'What's he want?'

'He wants you to bring your...guest out here, so he can take him home,' I said.

'Who died and made him King Shit,' she said. 'I don't answer to Northbridge meth dealers.' She leaned tighter into the rifle. 'I fucking waste them.'

Brave or psycho? Either way, she was holding her nerve better than me. My insides had liquified and threatened to trickle straight down onto my sneakers.

'Nobody's going to do anything stupid out here on the street,' I said. 'Plus, Bon and the others will be back soon.'

'Is that right...' said Viaspa, his voice thick with sarcasm.

About then I hit full panic mode. What did he know that I didn't?

'Angel,' my voice wavered. 'Give him what he wants.'

'Fuck off,' she retorted.

Cass began to shake. I wanted to hug her fear away, but the barrel jabbing into my skull gave a different set of instructions, and her fear was thoroughly justified.

It was dark enough for Viaspa to abduct me without a worry. If there were no gunshots, it just looked like a bunch of people congregating around the gate.

I heard a car purr up alongside the kerb.

'Well?' croaked Viaspa.

Angel didn't hesitate. 'Take her. And if you come around here again, I'll blow your balls off.'

My insides officially introduced themselves to my outsides. 'Fine,' I managed to spit out. 'But the girl stays here.' I gave Cass a big shove inside the gate towards the Nom holding a pistol.

As I moved, Viaspa yanked me backwards and I fell onto the pavement. The gate slammed shut and I was suddenly out there on my own with him. I rolled and got to my knees in one movement.

Viaspa stood backed up next to the open car door. I didn't have to see his face to know he was pissed off and embarrassed. He'd expected I'd be worth more to the

Cheaters than I was. And he hadn't banked on having to deal with Angel.

'Get in the car before I fuck you up right here,' he said.

His car was idling ready to go, and another sedan pulled up behind it. They were definitely the two cars I'd seen earlier. And there was no way I was getting inside either of them so they could drop me into the Serpentine Dam. I'd rather die here on the street, making all the noise, and pointing all the blame I could. 'Thanks for the offer,' I said. 'But it's been a long night.'

I straightened and began to slowly back away. My chest felt bruised as if it had been a training bag for a heavyweight boxing champion. I could hardly breathe.

Viaspa had his pistol resting close to his leg, pointing downward. To anyone peeping out their windows, into the darkened street, it would be impossible to see what he was holding. And anyway, I figured that the people living opposite the Cheaters compound were well practised in looking the other way.

Regardless of who might or might not intervene, now Cass was out of harm's way, I was not going to be compliant.

'Thanks for the offer,' I said. 'But it's been a long night.'

Viaspa stepped towards me threateningly. 'I've still got the little redhead, so you might want to think before you do anything stupid.'

Clemmie! I froze. *Crap!*

Now I had to go with him.

Then I had a flash. Clemmie had said Viaspa and Abramo were spooked by my abilities.

'Come any closer, and I'll cursssse your arssse,' I hissed a tad dramatically.

It seemed to work. He stopped and lowered his weapon.

'I mean it,' I said. 'Or I'll...I'll hex your...' I grappled around for a suitable threat, 'your drug pipeline.'

But my follow up threat seemed to have the reverse affect. Something...*Hex, who uses the word hex?*... jerked him free of his hesitation, and he began advancing again.

'Vieni!' he called loudly.

The driver and passenger from the second car jumped out and headed towards us.

I glanced to the cameras along the compound fence. Were they watching me on the CCTV, or had they gone back to rolling out swags?

Either way, pretty soon I'd be caught in a headlock and bundled into a boot for a short trip to some deep water. It was now or never.

So, I turned and sprinted away up the street, hoping they wouldn't shoot.

All three bunched up together to chase me. But I was quicker than they expected.

When they cleared the second car, I pulled a sharp change of direction and circumnavigated in a wide arc back to the first car. Soon as I got past it, I leapt into the open passenger side of the second car, slamming the door shut behind me, and rolled over to the driver's side. When that door was shut too, I hit the lock button, and took a shuddering breath.

They were only a second behind me, puffing, and thumping on the bonnet and roof.

Viaspa took off his jacket to wrap his pistol in it. He was going to break the window.

I pushed the ignition button and my heart lifted. It was keyless, but the starter was close enough for it to kick over.

I reversed out of there like a stunt car driver, and then jammed the stick in drive, before speeding away down the street. A quick check in the rear-view mirror showed them scrambling into the first car to follow. I zig-zagged through a couple lanes hoping to lose them. Something in the boot bumped around as I careened around corners.

Probably the weights they planned to drown me with.

Hands trembling, tears, streaming, I fumbled for my phone and hit the speed dial for Wal. When he answered, I almost bawled.

'Tara?'

'I stole Viaspa's car. He's chasing me. I'm just coming up on Lefty's.'

He knew me well enough to ask only the most important questions. 'How many of them?'

'Three. They used Cass to try and get into the compound. I got her free of them, but I think they might have Clemmie too.'

'Pull into Lefty's carpark now and come straight into the front bar. Make sure they see you do it.'

'That means I have to slow down.'

'Then slow down. Only enough until they see you, then hike it inside.'

'Wal?'

'Trust me.'

'ETA three minutes,' I yelped. Heart thundering, I took my foot off the pedal and slowed right down. It meant fighting every instinct to flee.

Thankfully traffic was light, and I had no one on my tail pushing me along.

As soon as I spotted them turn into the street, I

waited long enough for them to see me, and I floored the accelerator again. Two blocks later, I careened into the entrance of Lefty's, through the empty bottle shop drive-thru and right over to the carpark I'd been in a few hours earlier.

The lights were all out. The pub was closed. The carpark was deserted aside from a van and Mona.

I slotted in between the two vehicles, rolled out the door, and did the quickest ten-metre sprint ever not recorded.

They were parking their cars as I burst into the front bar.

The door was unlocked, but the room sat in utter darkness, aside from the bar fridge lights and a dull neon sign over the dart board.

I pulled up short for a moment, blind in the dark, trying to remember the configuration of the tables and the path through them, but everything was blobby and grey.

Then a hand gripped my shoulder and reefed me sideways.

'Shush!' said a voice in my ear, as I was folded under a smelly, sweaty armpit. *Bon Ames.*

My heartbeats clattered against my chest as I tried to quieten my breathing.

Then the door flung open and Viaspa and his guys entered.

'Bitch, we'll find you,' he called into the dark.

I held my breath, terrified for what was about to happen. Viaspa had a pistol. Where was Wal? What about Clemmie? Half formed thoughts buzzed around in my brain.

And then the lights flicked on.

Seconds passed before I could make sense of the scene.

I saw Cheaters, a dozen or more, on one side of the room.

Dennis and some Tenners on the other. They filled the gaps between tables, in a menacing formation, facing straight at Johnny V and his two guys by the door.

Every single person in the room was armed. Pistols, knives, rifles. One of Johnny's guys had a baseball bat. Had that been meant for me?

Bon shoved me to one side as Strange stepped forward into the tense silence and took the floor.

'What's going on, John?'

Viaspa stood stiff as a board, his aura pulsing around him in ugly pus-coloured bursts of heightened emotion. He pointed to me. 'Just some unfinished business with the girl.'

The girl? Seriously?

'You mean *our* girl,' Strange replied.

Suddenly all eyes were on me. I tried really hard not to squirm but failed. And the most uncomfortable of all was the piercing gaze from Dennis.

What the heck were Cheaters and Tenners doing in a room together...alive? Last I'd seen, they were about to go to war.

'You tried to break into my place when I wasn't there,' added Strange quietly. 'Dangerous move.'

'Not breaking in. Just an exchange. Her for my man, Abramo. We heard you had him. But it turns out your old lady didn't think she was worth it.'

Strange's expression didn't move, but I sensed his anger deepen. 'What makes you think we have him?'

'People talk,' John said, in an offhanded way. His aura began to change colour. I'd never seen that happen before. It took on a dull red glow, like molten lava.

Dennis moved over to stand alongside Strange. 'What kind of people?'

Viaspa held his pistol steady. 'Hey, I got no interest in your business, boys. We'll take this up with your girl another time. Just look after my man until we straighten it out.'

'Who ratted?' asked Dennis, insistently.

It felt like the bikers all took a step forward, closing in on Viaspa's guys, but no one actually moved.

Viaspa shrugged. 'Just some low life.' Though his words were dismissive, his aura shot out little eruptions that told me he was lying.

Who could he be protecting…? I ran through possible answers and took a punt. Clemmie's and my safety depended on it being the right one. 'Check their car,' I said.

'Explain,' said Strange without looking at me.

'Their snitch. He's in one of the car boots.'

Strange nodded to Bon Ames. He showed no hesitation in listening to me.

The man-mountain-peak tapped two of his men and they headed out the back exit.

'You gonna listen to this mouthy piece of work?" John called after them. 'What are you all? Pussy whipped?'

But his goading fell on deaf ears.

Instead, Viaspa's aura eruptions got worse as we waited. He began to visibly sweat.

So did I, praying I was right.

When Bon returned minutes later, he came in the front door, right behind John and his men.

'Move!' he barked.

They shuffled sideways, and Bon Ames sent Taco sprawling into the space at Strange and Dennis's feet.

Strange's face soured. And Dennis was looking at me again.

I didn't have to explain anything to anyone. Taco had been playing all sides, spying for Viaspa, and they knew it.

Strange addressed John. 'Piss off. Now. Before I forget our deal.'

Deal? What deal?

John began to back up towards the door, while casting me a filthy look.

'Wait!' I said. 'He's taken a young girl, Clemmie. Abramo was beating on her, and she came to me for help.'

Bon Ames immediately moved to block their exit.

'Where's this girl?' Strange demanded.

'What do you care? This is between us.' Viaspa motioned his head to include me.

'You're a dinosaur, John.' Strange said calmly. 'Men who abuse women have no place among us.'

Viaspa's mouth fell open in such unabashed surprise that even the corner of Dennis's mouth kinked.

'So...where is she?' asked Strange.

'With a friend.'

Strange nodded. 'Put your gun down and make the call.'

Slowly. So very slowly, Viaspa put his gun on the floor and reached into his pocket. He spoke a few curt words, instructing whoever was at the other end to put Clemmie in an Uber.

We all stood in suspended silence for a long while, until my phone finally rang.

Strange's eyes didn't move off Viaspa as he spoke to me. 'Answer it.'

I put the phone to my ear. 'Clemmie?'

'Tara? Where's Cass?'

'Safe. And you?'

'They put me in an Uber to your address.'

Jees, they know my address. Of course, they do. She sounded all right. Confused, maybe. But not terrified. 'Lock the doors. We'll be home in a while,' I said.

I clicked off and nodded at Strange.

'Beat it, John!' he said.

Viaspa puffed his chest up for a moment, then thought better of it.

Bon Ames stepped aside, and John and his men slid out the door.

That left the rest of us. And Taco.

Strange and Dennis exchanged such quietly spoken words, I couldn't hear them. Then Strange turned and walked out the back way. As his men followed, I got hauled along in their wake by Wal.

Looks like the Tenners got the pleasure of dealing with Taco.

Out in the back carpark, I began to shiver and shake like I was the aftershock of a scale seven earthquake.

'Bring her back to the club,' Bon Ames growled to Wal. 'We need to talk. And drink.'

Chapter Eleven

Tara

Soon after, I found myself at the Cheaters' rec-room bar drinking whisky and ice with Strange, Angel, Wal, and Bon Ames. Cass lay curled up on a couch asleep. And most of the others had bedded down in the swags and camp beds or were outside smoking and drinking.

My shakes had stopped after the fourth shot, and I sent Clemmie a text to check in. 'I'm going to go,' I said, stirring my bones from the stool.

'You should stay here tonight,' said Strange. 'Club rule when there's been friction.'

But Angel's sour expression said something different. *You're not one of us.*

And nor did I want to be!

Her abrupt departure to the other side of the room to collect glasses made her point even more strongly.

'Nah, I'm good. Wal and I'll grab Cass and go,' I replied.

Bon Ames stood up and belched. 'Right then. Gotta take a piss. I'll be in touch,' he said and wandered off.

'I'll call the Uber and wake Cass,' said Wal. He sculled the last of his drink and headed over to the sleeping girl.

That left Strange and I alone.

'How did you know it was Taco,' he asked softly.

I stared across the room to avoid his engulfing gaze. 'I didn't really. But I could see by Viaspa's reaction that the snitch was someone valuable to him. There was only one person who fitted that.'

'What was his reaction?'

I glanced briefly into his dark eyes and saw curiosity and respect. Then I looked away again. 'You saw it too. The sweating and such. I'm just more...attuned...to reading people quickly. The signs are clearer to me.'

He inhaled deeply and let it out in a controlled exhale. A meditation breath. 'You undersell your gift, Tara.'

I smiled inwardly, remembering my first conversation with Dennis. *Except when I don't.* 'Say, did you mean what you said to John? About men who abuse women not having a place with the Cheaters?'

'Have you met Angel?' He grinned at me. Like, really grinned. 'You think she'd put up with that?'

'You have a point,' I said.

We sipped in silence.

'And now we're good, right?' I suddenly wanted to go home and never see another bikie again. Ever.

He reached out and touched my shoulder. Kind of a friendly tap, mixed with something more proprietary.

'Oh, we're so good,' he replied, 'that I'm gonna patch you in.'

Chapter Twelve

Tara

Wal drove us home. I sat next to him, numb with exhaustion and the memory of Strange's last words to me. 'Wal, have you ever heard of a woman being patched in to a bikie group?' I said quietly.

He glanced sideways at me. The day was showing on him too. His eyes were hooded, and he slumped over the wheel. 'Not in this country. Dunno about the rest. Why?'

I sat in silence, letting him work it out.

After a while of watching the streaming streetlights and the slick blur of the Swan River at night, we rolled quietly into the carpark at home.

Neither of us moved.

Wal turned to me and offered me a smoke.

I nearly said yes. Not a smoker, but in that moment, it felt like I should be.

'Patch you in, eh? That's a big call. Won't be a popular one,' he said.

'Can't I just say no?'

He shrugged his shoulders, at a loss. 'Never heard of nothin' like it before. If you say no, someone'll likely do you for it. They got rules around that stuff. They don't like it when you turn 'em down.'

'Great.' Glum didn't even begin to describe my mood.

Wal took a drag on his Sobranie and puffed it out the window. 'Looks like you got a bigger problem than I thought.'

Before I could reply, our back door flung open, and the sound of raised voices flooded out. A moment later, two figures stepped out into the carpark. Their body language, even in the dark, was antagonistic. One towering over the other.

I recognised them both instantly. Ed and Nick.

'Oh yeah, Wal.' I replied. 'I surely do.'

About the Author

Marianne Delacourt is the pseudonym of a successful Australian sci-fi fantasy author who is sold throughout the world. *Sharp Shooter* and *Sharp Turn* are set in Perth, where the author grew up. *Too Sharp*, book three in the Tara Sharp series, is set in Brisbane where Marianne now lives.

Also from *deadlines*

Deadlines is the crime imprint of the award-winning Twelfth Planet Press specialty small press. We aim to promote quality, fun writing in fresh, exciting projects that seeks to raise the awareness of women's voices, and demonstrate the depth and breadth of Australian fiction to a broader audience.

Tara Sharp

Sharp Shooter

Sharp Turn

Too Sharp

Sharp Edge

Razor Sharp

Café La Femme
by Livia Day

A Trifle Dead

The Blackmail Blend (ebook)

Drowned Vanilla

Keep Calm & Kill the Chef

www.twelfthplanetpress.com

Tara Sharp Book One

Marianne Delacourt

Available in paperback, ebook and in audio on Audible

Tara Sharp should be just another unemployable, twenty-something, ex-private schoolgirl ... but she has the gift—or curse as she sees it—of reading people's auras. The trouble is, auras sometimes tell you things about people they don't want you to know.

When a family friend recommends Mr Hara's Paralanguage School, Tara decides to give it a whirl—and graduates with flying colours. So when Mr Hara picks up passes on a job for a hot-shot lawyer she jumps at the chance despite some of his less-than-salubrious clients.

Tara should know better than to get involved when she learns the job involves mob boss Johnny Vogue. But she's broke and the magic words 'retainer' and 'bonus' have been mentioned. Soon Tara finds herself sucked into an underworld 'situation' that has her running for her life.

Winner of the Davitt Award for Best Crime Novel and nominated for a Ned Kelly Award for Best First Crime novel. Killer Nashville Silver Falchion Finalist

Tara Sharp Book Two

Marianne Delacourt

Available in paperback, ebook and in audio on Audible

Tara's quirky PI business is attracting some even quirkier customers. She's not sure how Madame Vine's Escort Agency got her number. And then there's the eccentric motorcycle racing team owner, Bolo Ignatius. Both these clients want to Tara to investigate suspicious circumstances that turn up dead bodies. That can only mean one thing in this town: John Viaspa. Tara goes in for round two with the local crime boss, while balancing the tight rope of her deliciously complicated love life.

Tara Sharp's life can only be describe as furious fun.

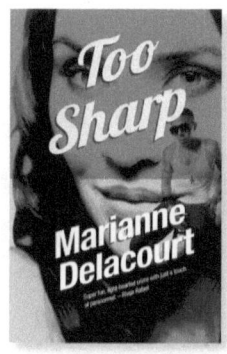

Too Sharp

Tara Sharp Book Three

Marianne Delacourt

Available in paperback, ebook and in audio on Audible

Tara Sharp's new case brings her to Brisbane, where she is placed in charge of Slim Sledge, a high-maintenance rock star. Tara's a sucker for a backstage pass, and it'll provide some much-needed distance between herself and her mother's not-so-subtle hints about getting a 'real' job, not to mention crime lord Johnny Viaspa, the only man on the planet who wants her dead.

She expected the music industry to be cut-throat, but Tara soon uncovers more problems than just Slim Sledge's demands and his rabid fans. Everywhere she turns, the grudges run deeper and the danger ramps up.

Has Tara finally pushed her luck too far?

Tara Sharp Book Four

Marianne Delacourt

Available in paperback, ebook and in audio on Audible

Dead bodies, a complicated love life, a conflict between the local drug cartels, and a favour owed to the local bikies have Tara scrambling to stay ahead of the game.

Just another Tuesday for Tara Sharp

Book 1 in *The Café La Femme* series

Livia Day

Availiable in paperback and ebook

Tabitha Darling has always had a dab hand for pastry and a knack for getting into trouble. Which was fine when she was a tearaway teen, but not so useful now she's trying to run a hipster urban cafe, invent the perfect trendy dessert, and stop feeding the many (oh so unfashionable) policemen in her life.

When a dead muso is found in the flat upstairs, Tabitha does her best (honestly) not to interfere with the investigation, despite the cute Scottish blogger who keeps angling for her help. Her superpower is gossip, not solving murder mysteries, and those are totally not the same thing, right?

But as that strange death turns into a string of random crimes across the city of Hobart, Tabitha can't shake the unsettling feeling that maybe, for once, it really is ALL ABOUT HER.

And maybe she's figured out the deadly truth a trifle late...

Shortlisted for Best Debut Book, Davitt Award for Australian Women's Crime Writing and a Killer Nashville Silver Falchion Finalist